CHARLIE NUMB3RS
and **the woolly mammoth**

Also by Ben and Tonya Mezrich

Bringing Down the Mouse
Charlie Numbers and the Man in the Moon

THE CHARLIE NUMBERS ADVENTURES

CHARLIE NUMB3RS

and the woolly mammoth

WITHDRAWN

BEN and TONYA MEZRICH

Simon & Schuster Books for Young Readers

NEW YORK   LONDON   TORONTO   SYDNEY   NEW DELHI

SIMON & SCHUSTER BOOKS FOR YOUNG READERS
An imprint of Simon & Schuster Children's Publishing Division
1230 Avenue of the Americas, New York, New York 10020

SIMON & SCHUSTER BOOKS FOR YOUNG READERS
is a trademark of Simon & Schuster, Inc.
For information about special discounts for bulk purchases, please contact Simon & Schuster Special Sales at 1-866-506-1949 or business@simonandschuster.com.
The Simon & Schuster Speakers Bureau can bring authors to your live event. For more information or to book an event, contact the Simon & Schuster Speakers Bureau at 1-866-248-3049 or visit our website at www.simonspeakers.com.
Jacket design by Krista Vossen
Interior design by Hilary Zarycky
The text for this book was set in Life LT Std.
Manufactured in the United States of America
1019 FFG
First Edition
2 4 6 8 10 9 7 5 3 1
Library of Congress Cataloging-in-Publication Data
Names: Mezrich, Ben, 1969– author. | Mezrich, Tonya, author.
Title: Charlie Numbers and the woolly mammoth / Ben and Tonya Mezrich.
Description: First edition. | New York : Simon & Schuster Books for Young Readers, [2019] | Summary: Sixth-grade mathematical genius Charlie Lewis, the Whiz Kids, and new friends follow their hunch that eccentric billionnaire Blake Headstrom is importing mammoth tusks for sinister purposes.
Identifiers: LCCN 2018049877|
ISBN 9781534441002 (hardcover) | ISBN 9781534441026 (eBook)
Subjects: | CYAC: Mathematics—Fiction. | Genius—Fiction. | Woolly mammoth—Fiction. | Mammoths—Fiction. | Smuggling—Fiction. | Boston (Mass.)—Fiction. | Mystery and detective stories.
Classification: LCC PZ7.M5753 Cm 2019 | DDC [Fic]—dc23
LC record available at https://lccn.loc.gov/2018049877

To Arya and Asher—you may be little, but your curiosity inspires us every day in large ways

Acknowledgments

This third adventure with Charlie was a dream come true for me. Continuing his story with the Whiz Kids would not have been possible without the support and care from my editor, David Gale, and his team at Simon & Schuster Books for Young Readers, especially Amanda Ramirez.

To our agents, Eric Simonoff and Matt Snyder: you shine a bright light on our pathway every day. To my dear friends from dental school who stood by us for Charlie's adventures, Elena Friedman, Titi Dang, and Daniel Friedman: you guys mean the world to us. Ellen Pompeo, Chris Ivery, and Laura Holstein at Calamity Jane, we are thrilled to have you bring Charlie to the screen.

To our Boston Family—you know who you are—thank you for believing in Charlie and his message. Especially Dr. George Church for welcoming us with open arms into his lab and life, and Dawn and Harper Oates for being an inspiration to us all. A warm thank-you to my parents, Ron and Fu-mei Chen, who always taught me that science and math were extremely important subjects. I owe it to you for giving me that strong foundation and always putting education first with me and my three incredible siblings, Tree, Oliver, and Sonya.

And last but not least, thank you, Ben, for always believing in me and being my rock and my sounding board, both when times are tough and when times are easy. And to Asher and Arya for inspiring me to chase my dreams and be the best mommy I can be.

—T. M.

1

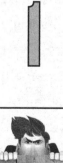

CHARLIE LEWIS BRACED HIMSELF against the rocking of the deck beneath his feet, as the cold metal railing pressed into his lower back. He'd never been great with boats, or, for that matter, water in general. He wasn't much of a swimmer, and he couldn't catch a fish to save his life. The fact that he was now standing on a cargo ship parked at a dockyard in Boston Harbor, rollicking and rolling above choppy waves as high as Charlie was tall, made him question every decision he'd made over the past few weeks—if not every decision he'd made over the past twelve years.

It certainly didn't help that the remaining rays of winter sunlight were shining blindingly down. In the distance, he could barely make out the giant face of the clock tower, rising up above the pincushion of buildings that made up Boston's Financial District. The giant digital display told him it was five thirty in the afternoon, which meant Charlie should have been home from school already, maybe telling his mother about his day, or watching cartoons with his dad. Having professors for parents meant someone was usually home when he got out of his classes, and usually that was a good thing. But sometimes, like when things got seriously out of control, it meant when Charlie got home—if Charlie got home—he'd have a lot to explain.

Like how an otherwise normal Thursday late afternoon in February had gotten him here, to the very edge of a giant boat, his sneakers inches from the long drop down to the icy water of Boston Harbor.

The briny smell of the waves filled his nostrils as his mind began calculating the drop itself. The math wasn't hard—not nearly as difficult as keeping his balance as each wave pushed against the mammoth boat, sending it bouncing high in the air despite the ropes that tethered it to the dock. It was 60 feet to the water; 720 inches, 1,828.8 centimeters. Given enough time, Charlie could have calculated how fast he'd be going when he hit, even how much liquid his body would displace.

He'd always found comfort in the math, the numbers.

Numbers were concrete, something you could count, and count on. His affinity for numbers was so well known among his sixth-grade classmates that they'd attached the word to his name. Nobody had called him Charlie Lewis since fourth grade, when he'd aced a ninth-grade math test that had been handed out to his class by mistake: It was always Charlie "Numbers."

As he stood on the edge of the ship pondering the numbers, he suddenly caught sight of something moving behind a barrel down below, on the nearby pier. He could see the border of a red swing coat under a yellow neon vest and a mop of familiar auburn hair: Crystal Mueller and Jeremy "Diapers" Draper were hard to miss, despite their best efforts to remain hidden. Crystal, known for her vast knowledge of geology that far surpassed any high school student's, was the quasi coleader of the Whiz Kids. That was the de facto name of his squad of friends from Nagassack Middle School, the public school in Newton that served as home to Charlie and more than three hundred other students— the worst of whom had granted Charlie's best friend, Jeremy, with his inescapable nickname. Charlie would always remember the day his friend had transformed from Jeremy Draper to Jeremy Diapers: The school bully, Dylan Wigglesworth, had tripped Jeremy, who'd then inadvertently emptied out his ever-present back-pack all over the cafeteria, revealing his baby sister's disposables instead of his science project.

Looking down at Jeremy and Crystal in their fairly awful hiding places, Charlie realized that—no matter how close they were—he was still on his own. Jeremy and Crystal might as well have been all the way across town.

So, instead, he let the numbers do their magic; he began to calculate. Not just the distance to the water, but suddenly *everything* became numbers—the height of the ship, the depth of the harbor, the density of the water, the temperature of the air. As his mind ran through the calculations, he absentmindedly glanced down at his hands, at the curved white object he held as it caught the sunlight, flashing almost as bright as a star.

Charlie looked up from the object and again found the clock tower in the distance. The display had shifted from time to temperature: The city of Boston was registering a blustery thirty-six degrees. Charlie knew that thirty-six degrees Fahrenheit was slightly above freezing, but mathematically still cold enough to illicit hypothermia; a human body hitting water at that temperature would have only a few minutes, even less if that human body happened to be the size of an average third grader.

And the water of the harbor had to be many degrees colder than the ambient air.

"Not a good idea, kid. You might survive the drop, but not for very long."

The voice cracked through the air like a leather belt pulled tight. Charlie looked back and saw a large, trash-can-shaped man coming toward him across the deck, followed by a second man, stringy and tall, dressed in green.

"Popsicle city, kid," the second man added, grinning. His teeth were crooked and yellow, like thirty-year-old Pez lost for decades in the bottom of a drawer.

Charlie turned away from the men, forcing himself to go back to the math. Back to his calculations: distance, weight, temperature. How his exact body weight—fifty-eight pounds—would interact with the water, how much time he'd have before frostbite hit.

"Just hand it over," the trash can of a man said, still moving closer. "Give it to us, and this doesn't have to get ugly."

Charlie inhaled deeply, the saltiness of the ocean palpable in his throat. Then he looked down again at the object in his hands. The object felt smooth and cold and heavy against his palms. He knew that if he handed it to the men, they probably would let him go. After all, without the object—without that important piece of evidence—he was just some kid that nobody would believe. Without evidence, he had nothing but a story. Wild, incredible, terrifying—but just a story.

Charlie shook his head. He had come this far. Too far. And people were counting on him. His friends were counting on him.

His friends.

And then he paused, a sudden thought trickling through the fear in his head. He balanced the heavy object against his chest with one hand, and reached into his pocket with the other.

His fingers closed against a cool plastic tube—and his mind started to whirl. *Could it work? Was it possible?*

He made a sudden decision, and mashed the tube with his fist, squirting the clear jelly inside all over his palm. Then he quickly yanked his hand out of his pocket, and began rubbing the stuff on his cheeks, forehead, neck, his hands and wrists—any exposed flesh—in as thick a layer as he could.

"What the heck are you doing?" the man in green asked, through a cruel laugh. "You don't need sunscreen where you're thinking of going."

Charlie ignored the voice. He knew it was a long shot, but it was all he had.

As a cold breeze touched his cheeks, he grasped the object in his hand even tighter, then focused on the water—and the long drop down.

"Kid, don't! You're crazy!" one of the men shouted.

"I might be crazy," Charlie said, "but I never miscalculate."

He stepped forward off the edge of the deck, and suddenly he was plummeting toward the icy water below.

Two Weeks Earlier . . .

A THIN FROSTING OF snow blanketed the ground beneath Charlie's feet as he rubbed his hands together for warmth. He'd forgotten to bring his gloves, but then again, he hadn't expected to be spending most of the afternoon outside, in a quiet corner of the Boston Public Garden, watching one of his friends crouched down on hands and knees, digging at the half-frozen ground as if his life depended on it.

"You really think a pen is the best tool for something like this?" Charlie asked.

Marion Tuttle didn't look up from his work. He'd done a pretty good job of clearing the snow away from the two-foot-square area in front of him that he'd designated as square one in his excavation efforts, but now that he had actually reached dirt, the job had gotten much more difficult. To that end, he'd retrieved a Bic pen from the pocket of his bulky down jacket and was now jabbing and stabbing at the ground, throwing up chunks of mud, dead grass, and gravel.

"Are you even sure you're looking in the right place?" Jeremy Draper added from a few feet behind Charlie. "The way you were juggling those things, it could have gone ten feet in any direction."

Marion shot a look toward Jeremy, then went right back to his digging. Jeremy was grinning beneath his mop of bright red hair; he was enjoying this, mainly because, this time, it wasn't his fault. Although Jeremy, Charlie's best friend, was notoriously clumsy—the fault of his overly tall, elongated body, pipe-cleaner-thin arms and legs—it wasn't Jeremy who had decided that the class trip to Boston's oldest park would be a good time to show off his juggling skills. And it wasn't Jeremy who had made the potentially fatal mistake of using a trio of stones from Crystal Mueller's legendary rock collection, some of which she carried with her at all times, as juggling props.

If looks could kill, Marion would have needed to dig a much bigger hole than the one he was working on. Crystal was glaring at him from the other side of Charlie, her eyes on fire behind her Coke-bottle-thick glasses. He knew if he didn't find the piece of tanzanite he'd lost in the wind, or the sun, or to his own thick and fumbling lack of agility, he was going to end up buried right next to her prize bit of geology.

"Maybe next time you should just try shooting a bow and arrow with your feet while riding on the back of a horse," Kentaro Mori said from next to Crystal.

Even Crystal had to smile at that one. All five of them— Charlie and his group of hyperintelligent best friends— had visited the Big Apple Circus the week before. Charlie's dad had gotten the tickets half price from MIT, where he taught physics; maybe he'd hoped that seeing contortionists, dog trainers, and trapeze artists would inspire Charlie and his friends to focus on something other than their schoolwork, at least for a few days. But the circus, and especially the juggling act, should have come with a warning: Don't Try This at Home.

Especially if you were Marion Tuttle, whose doughy physique and plump fingers left Charlie wondering how the kid was such an incredible artist. He could sketch just about anything to near perfection, and create some of the coolest digital masterpieces that their art teachers had ever seen.

But the skills of an artist didn't translate to juggling.

"Maybe one of you guys can help out, instead of

standing around making jokes?" Marion said, then sneezed, so loudly that it startled a family of tourists moving down one of the nearby paths.

As Marion sneezed a second time, Charlie looked past the family and could just barely make out the rest of their classmates, a good thirty feet beyond where they were huddled around Marion. The fact that the rest of their class hadn't noticed that the Whiz Kids had remained behind when they followed the pair of teachers in charge of the class trip to the next stop on their tour of the Public Garden wasn't surprising. After all, the only time the other kids at Nagassack Middle paid attention to Charlie and his friends was when the Whiz Kids were facing off with one of the school's handful of bullies. More often than not it was Dylan Wigglesworth—the bane of Charlie's life at Nagassack, a pituitary case of a kid built like a linebacker—and his pair of thugs, Liam and Dusty. But even Dylan hadn't noticed the Whiz Kids breaking off from the larger group.

Then again, the Boston Public Garden was pretty enough to distract even the most brutish of sixth graders. Founded in 1837, the Garden had been constructed over salvaged marshland adjacent to the much larger, and similarly as old, Boston Common. It was considered frillier than its neighbor, with sinewy pathways and a suspension bridge that crossed over a kidney-shaped pond. There, during summer months, pedal-powered Swan Boats mingled with families of Canada geese, and a pair of transplanted swans, in an iconic Garden that had served as an urban oasis for generations of Bostonians.

During the first part of their field trip, Charlie and his friends had learned that much of the Garden had remained unchanged since the Victorian era, from the cast-iron fence that surrounded the plot land to the old gas lamps that ran along the paths, which had run with real gas until the late nineteenth century. Only on closer inspection had Charlie noticed that the lamps were now electric—and in fact many of them had also been fitted with tiny surveillance cameras by the Boston Parks Department, most likely to cut down on a recent spike in late-night petty crime. Although the cameras seemed anachronistic in such a historic spot, Charlie was comforted to know that someone had an eye on what was going on—though if they were watching now, all they'd see was a chubby redhead digging in the dirt with a pen, while sneezing up a storm.

"Seriously, are you allergic to snow, too?" Crystal said, finally breaking her silence. "Is that even possible?"

Marion's food allergies were well known among his crew. The Whiz Kids could rattle them off at a moment's notice, and took pride in doing so to wide-eyed waitstaff whenever they were trying out a new restaurant: coconut, shellfish, gluten, nuts, and a slew of other obscure food items, from cilantro to sesame seeds. Not to mention the more common nonfood allergens like dust, dog hair, and grass.

Marion sneezed again, then hit the ground even more furiously, using the pen with both hands to dig even deeper. Piles of frozen soil were building up next to where he was kneeling, but there was still no sign of Crystal's tanzanite.

"Guys," Charlie said, "I think this is hopeless. We'd better join the rest of the class before someone realizes we're gone—"

He was interrupted by the sudden look that had crossed Crystal's face; her eyes had gone wide as saucers, and she was staring at the dirt beneath Marion's jabbing pen.

"Hold on," she said, stepping forward.

"Is it your rock?" Jeremy asked.

Charlie peered over Marion's shoulder as Crystal got down on her knees next to their artistic friend.

Something shiny and white and pointy was peeking up out of the hole he had just dug.

"That's not tanzanite," Crystal said.

"Is it ice?" Kentaro asked.

It was certainly shiny and white, but it didn't look like ice. Charlie lowered himself to his knees as well, as both Crystal and Marion began digging even harder and faster. As they dug, it became apparent that whatever they had found was bigger than it had first appeared— the white point was the tip of something that went down into the dirt.

"I think it's oblong," Crystal said.

"What does that mean?" Jeremy asked.

"Elongated, curved or rectangular," Kentaro said. He was the linguist of the group, speaking more languages than the rest of them combined.

Charlie narrowed his eyes as more of the object was revealed. It was indeed curved and white, but it had a familiar shape. When, finally, Marion and Crystal got it fully out of the dirt, Crystal pulling it gingerly with her fingers and then placing it on the ground next to the piles Marion had unearthed, Charlie was able to estimate the object's size: nine inches, tip to tip, curved like one of those swords from a pirate movie. Except it definitely wasn't a sword, or anything man made. And the white material wasn't metal or stone or plastic—it looked kind of like bone.

"This doesn't look like it's supposed to be here," Crystal mused. "And it looks old. Really old."

"Do you think this is—well . . . ," Jeremy started.

Charlie finished the thought for him.

"A bone? From, like, an animal?"

"But why is it buried in the Public Garden?" asked Marion.

Charlie had a disturbing thought.

"I read somewhere that it's rumored that human bones were unearthed by the electric company years ago when they were digging the subway under the Common," he said. "Could this be something like that?"

Crystal moved a few inches back from the object, her lips turning down at the corners.

"You think this could be a human bone?"

Charlie swallowed, then looked up, across the park toward the rest of their class, who were now gathered at the far edge of the Public Garden, by a parade of bronze statues of a family of ducks—a permanent installation that had been built as an homage to a classic children's book by Robert McCloskey about eight baby ducks that followed their mother into the park, looking for a home. Charlie could still remember some of the baby ducks' names: Mack, Quack, Ouack, etc. As a little kid, he'd sat upon those statues many times during family outings, usually around the holidays.

He turned back to Crystal.

"I don't know. All I can say is that it doesn't seem like it was purposefully buried here. Look at how shallow this dirt is, Marion's pen didn't get him very deep."

"So, the object looks old," Crystal said, "but it wasn't buried very long ago."

Charlie nodded. Then he made a decision. They hadn't found Crystal's tanzanite—but maybe they'd found something even more interesting. It was certainly something worth investigating further.

They weren't the cool kids at school. Far from it. But the fact that they could solve mysteries by using their mental tools gave them a sense of purpose, and made Charlie feel special. Science didn't care if you were cool; science only cared that you were right.

"We can't just leave this here, to get buried again by the snow."

"So what should we do with it?" Marion asked. "How do we figure out what it is?"

Charlie smiled.

"I think I know where we should start."

HER NAME WAS MABEL, and she had been standing guard over the science lab at Nagassack Middle School for as long as anyone could remember.

Her frail body hung silently at the entrance to the second-floor classroom, her arms, legs, hands, and feet connected to her torso by clear plastic wires, nearly invisible to the naked eye. Because it was winter, a red-and-white Santa hat was perched on her startling white head, and around her neck hung a matching striped wool scarf. At Halloween, which the kids knew was her season, she wore a witch's hat and a skeleton mask. Mrs. Hennigan, the science teacher who lorded over the second-floor lab like a queen over her territory, thought it was funny for a skeleton to wear a skeleton mask, but to the kids at Nagassack, it was just plain weird.

But then again, almost everything about Mrs. Hennigan was weird. Her curly white hair billowed like clouds above her head, and she always wore thick blue eyeliner. The pantsuits and dresses she wore were the shape, color, and consistency of potato sacks. And she often lost her train of thought right in the middle of a sentence. Once, she'd walked right out of class halfway through a lecture on the circulatory system; when she finally reappeared, twenty minutes later, she had continued like nothing had happened, picking up between the left and right ventricles where she'd left off.

The only thing weirder in the science lab than Mrs. Hennigan was the lab's mascot, Mabel, which, she constantly reminded her students, was the second-most-expensive thing at Nagassack Middle School, after the state-of-the-art stereomicroscope on the back table by the windows.

And it was there—by that fancy, insect-shaped microscope, which would have been at home in a top-flight university—that Charlie found himself at eight fifteen the morning after the field trip to the Public Garden, hovering near Crystal, whose thick glasses were pressed right up against the tubular eyepieces of the device, as her fingers worked tiny metal knobs on either side. Jeremy and Marion were on either side of Charlie, standing so close that he could feel their warm breath next to each of his ears. Kentaro, the best talker of the group, was on the other side of the rectangular lab, keeping Mrs. Hennigan occupied; although the bell for first period wouldn't go off for another fifteen minutes, it would not have been unusual for Mrs. Hennigan to draft a group of students she happened upon in her lab to help her with some arcane experiment she was working on. Charlie had once almost missed his bus home from school assisting the science teacher on an autopsy of a flatworm. And today, Charlie and his friends couldn't risk being waylaid by the odd bird of a teacher. They had a mystery to solve.

As Crystal worked with the microscope, Charlie glanced back over his shoulder. Kentaro seemed to be doing a good job with Mrs. Hennigan; the two of them were still in Mabel's shadow, close to the door leading out into the hallway. Between Mabel and the microscope, the lab could easily fit thirty students: long metal tables lined up in the front half of the room, and lab benches beneath metal shelves housing a metropolis of scientific paraphernalia took up much of the back half of the room. Everything from test tubes to Bunsen burners, as well as a few items that were probably

unique to Mrs. Hennigan's brand: a preserved scor-
pion in liquid, two stuffed snakes, and a cabinet full of
insects in tiny jars. Because of the macabre collection,
the place smelled of formaldehyde, with a hint of wood
shavings, the kind you might find at the bottom of a
hamster cage.

"So have you figured out what it is?" Marion whispered toward Crystal, bringing Charlie's attention back
to the microscope and the object that was resting on the
tray beneath the device's telescoping lens.

Crystal's gaze remained unbroken. Her brow fur-
rowed behind her glasses, then her nose crinkled like
a rabbit sniffing for carrots. Charlie had seen that look
before, and he had to admit, it was kind of cute. He
shook his head to quickly erase the thought. Crystal
hated the word "cute," and had she known what he
was thinking, he would have ended up in one of Mrs.
Hennigan's specimen jars.

Although it had been Charlie's idea to use the microscope in the science lab to investigate the object they
had found in the Public Garden, it had been Crystal
who had been tasked with holding on to the sample
until that morning. She had managed to smuggle it
home from the field trip in her pink backpack without the trip proctors—or her parents, when they

had picked her up from the trip drop-off—noticing. Getting the object to school that morning had been a little trickier. Crystal's mom had been packing her backpack for her since kindergarten. But Crystal had realized that the mission was a perfect opportunity for her to assert some level of independence; in less than a year, she was going to be a teenager, and sooner or later, her mother was going to have to accept that Crystal was growing up.

Doing things on her own was a big part of growing up; sure, Charlie knew, they could have asked their parents for help with the mystery of the ivory-colored object, but it was something they would much rather figure out on their own.

"I believe it is some sort of bone," Crystal finally said, pulling back from the microscope.

"Bone?" squawked Jeremy, much too loud. "Are you sure? Like, as in, human bone?"

Crystal removed the sample from the microscope and held it up to the fluorescent light streaming from the lab's ceiling panels. She turned it back and forth, her eyes squinting behind her glasses. To Charlie, the whiteness of the curved object looked more yellowish than it had appeared outside; he wondered if that was a trick of the fluorescence, or if getting it inside, out of the cold, had revealed a little more of its true essence.

"You see these lines along the side of the object? They seem pretty straight to me. Human bone has a characteristic pattern of concentric circles, like a target, or a bull's-eye. So I don't think it's human—but I do think it's bone."

"Human bones have a pattern of concentric circles," Jeremy repeated. "Why do you know that?"

"I know lots of things," Crystal said. She was about to add more, but suddenly Kentaro was moving toward them, waving his arms around his head.

"Incoming! Incoming!" he screeched, but too late—Mrs. Hennigan was right behind him, clapping her hands together.

"Oh wonderful, so many assistants in my lab and we still have ten minutes before class! I just got in a shipment of frozen geckos. They're such wonderful lizards to dissect, and they should be almost thawed out—"

"Mrs. Hennigan," Charlie hastily interrupted, "we'd love to help out with your lizards, but we found something really interesting."

"More interesting than the intestines of a gecko?" Mrs. Hennigan said, shaking her head. "I can't imagine that's true. All I need is a few minutes to prepare the dissection table—"

"But, Mrs. Hennigan," Marion suddenly interrupted, "we have a hypothesis!" Hennigan froze—and then a smile moved across her face. Marion had used what passed for a magic word in Hennigan's lab. Since the first day of school, Hennigan had drilled every class she taught on the six steps of the scientific method: Ask a question, research, hypothesis, experiment, analyze and conclude, present results. It was something they had been forced to parrot in dozens of pop quizzes, on midterm exams, in homework papers.

"A hypothesis?" Mrs. Hennigan repeated.

Charlie quickly took the bait. He gingerly grabbed the bonelike object from Crystal and showed it to their teacher. Mrs. Hennigan's eyes grew wide as she leaned forward for a better look.

"We found it yesterday in the Public Garden," Charlie said.

"And we hypothesize," Jeremy butted in, hitting the magic word for almost comic emphasis, "that it's some sort of bone."

Mrs. Hennigan grinned.

"There may be hope for you yet, Mr. Draper. So you've got your hypothesis. And what's next, in the scientific method?"

"Experiment!" said Kentaro, nearly shouting.

"Analyze and conclude," added Charlie.

"Present results," finished Marion.

"If we're going to get to the bottom of this, it looks like we have our work cut out for us," replied Mrs. Hennigan.

Crystal pointed to the microscope. "It's just not powerful enough to tell us anything important."

Charlie knew that the stereomicroscope, as expensive as it was, could only magnify objects up to one hundred times their actual size. It worked by something called "incident light illumination," which basically meant it used the light reflected off the surface of a sample to enhance the size. Not only did it provide two separate viewing angles—the left and right eye, hence the prefix "stereo"—but the scope was also able to provide a pretty good 3-D visualization. But for truly identifying the object, 3-D and a hundred times magnification just weren't enough. They needed to go much, much deeper.

"I think I might have a solution," Mrs. Hennigan said—and suddenly she spun on her heel, so fast that her potato sack of a dress swept around her like the outer edge of a burlap tornado.

She rushed across the lab to a wooden desk just beyond Mabel's hanging skeletal heels. The desk was cluttered with files, papers, test tubes, and pipettes. Mrs. Hennigan dug through the mess, and then came back toward Charlie and his friends holding a rolled-up newspaper.

Reaching them, she unfolded the paper with a flourish. Charlie saw that it was the *Boston Globe*, and that it was open to a special science section, an insert that appeared in the daily local paper on a bimonthly basis.

On the cover of the section, halfway up the page, was a photo of a bearded man with wire-rimmed glasses. The man was standing in some sort of lab, and even from the photo, Charlie could tell that the man was extremely tall. His beard was white, matching his hair, and he looked a little bit like a thin, elongated version of Santa Claus. But instead of a red-and-white suit, or a hat like the one gracing Mabel's grinning skull, this Santa Claus was wearing a white lab coat.

"If anyone can give us a deeper look into what you've found," Mrs. Hennigan said, "it's this man."

Charlie looked closer, picking out the caption beneath the photo.

"Dr. George Church," Charlie read. "Is he a scientist?"

"He defines the term," Mrs. Hennigan said, and smiled, a twinkle in her eye. "He's one of the leading scientists of our time. A geneticist, a biologist—some call him a modern-day Einstein. And it just so happens he owes me a favor."

Charlie couldn't imagine how a prominent scientist could possibly owe Mrs. Hennigan anything, let alone a favor, but he wasn't about to turn down an opportunity to meet a modern-day Einstein. At best, they'd find the answers they were looking for, and figure out what, exactly, they'd found buried in the Public Garden.

At worst, a visit with Dr. George Church couldn't possibly be as bad as conducting an autopsy on a flatworm, or chopping their way into the intestines of a partially frozen reptile.

IT HAPPENED SO FAST, Charlie didn't have time to react. One minute he was standing next to a long metal table in one of the few open areas of Dr. Church's lab on the third floor of Harvard University's New Research Building, trying to calm his nerves as he waited for their esteemed "tour guide" to arrive. The next thing he knew he was falling backward, a plastic pipette filled with clear liquid spinning past him, just inches from his face.

He hit the floor shoulder first, then felt the splatter of cold liquid raining down as the pipette continued on its path, bouncing off the wall behind Charlie, then ricocheting back and landing right next to where he was lying.

Charlie looked up, shocked, and saw an olive-skinned

kid with jet-black hair peering down at him. The kid had to be half a foot taller than Charlie and, from below, might as well have been the size of a mountain.

"Wow, you really are a geek," the kid said, laughing. "Why don't you try catching it next time, instead of diving for cover. It was just filled with water. Not the Ebola virus."

Charlie's face turned red as Jeremy helped him back to his feet. The kid with the jet-black hair shook his head, still laughing, then crossed back to his friends—a group of four kids whom Charlie had met only moments before, when his own group had followed Mrs. Hennigan out of the elevators that led into the labyrinthine lab. Aside from the big Latino kid who had just floored Charlie, there was a petite African-American girl in a wheelchair, and two Indian boys who looked like they could be twins. Mrs. Hennigan had quickly gone around a corner to introduce herself to her counterpart—a thin man in a white oxford shirt, emblazoned with a crest from the King School, a gem of the Boston Public School System. They assumed he too was a science teacher, as Mrs. Hennigan and the stringy man nodded heads in acknowledgment of each other.

As the teachers continued to converse, the kids

were left to momentarily eye one another without adult supervision.

"Rod, leave him alone," said the girl in the wheel-chair. "We're all geeks here. It's a Saturday morning and we're in a Harvard lab. By choice, I might add."

The big kid—Rod—rolled his eyes.

"Janice, you have one heck of a soft spot for losers. Your collection of nerds is almost as big as your collection of fossils. And that's saying a lot."

Charlie tried to wipe the embarrassment from his face as he picked up the errant pipette. How was he supposed to have known that it was just filled with water? He was used to being made fun of, but he hadn't expected his visit to the Church Lab to have started with a pipette flying toward his head.

He sighed to himself; every school had its resident bully, and obviously the King School had Rod. Big—not muscled and bulky like Dylan Wigglesworth but a tower compared to Charlie—and smirking, the kid seemed to have a real chip on his shoulder. It was odd, that someone like him would have chosen to spend a Saturday morning at a lab, even if it was presided over by one of the greatest living scientists.

When Mrs. Hennigan had told Charlie and his friends that she had made good on her offer—exchanging the favor she was owed for a visit to the Church Lab—he had assumed they'd be meeting the scientist on their own. But, as Mrs. Hennigan had explained on the short bus ride over to the Harvard New Research Building in Brookline, for the past year the Church Lab had been reaching out to local schools in an effort to get more kids interested in the biological sciences. Kids from all over the area were being invited to bring in objects they found in the environment for study—and Dr. Church had squeezed in Mrs. Hennigan's request along with a scheduled visit from the King School.

Janice Netoyer, the girl in the wheelchair, seemed to be the leader of the crew that had greeted them when they'd first entered the lab. She was small for her age, with hair pulled tightly against her head in elaborate braids, tied off with tiny pink elastics. She was wearing a matching pink skirt, and Charlie could see a blanket covering her legs. Although she was petite, she appeared to have abundant energy, and seemed able to control the much bigger Rod with a single look.

She maneuvered her chair around a low counter covered in test-tube racks, stopping a few feet in front of where Charlie was still dusting himself off.

"Sorry about the rough introduction. Rod can be a

handful, but if he had a heart, I think it would be in the right place."

Rod rolled his eyes, then stalked off to play with a metal scale by a washing station near the far wall. The two Indian kids followed Rod, leaving Janice alone with Charlie and his friends.

"This is pretty cool, isn't it?" Janice asked.

She deftly turned her chair as if surveying the lab that extended out in random directions from where they were standing, like the narrow strands of an intricate spiderweb. If Mrs. Hennigan hadn't led Charlie from the elevator, he would have gotten lost a dozen times before finding the spot by himself. Charlie had no idea how many people worked in the lab, but along the way, he'd passed a dozen people in lab coats and safety goggles, hovering over various pieces of machinery that Charlie couldn't even begin to identify. Crystal had called out the things she'd recognized—"A chemical scale!" "A centrifuge!"—as if she were on some sort of game show, but even she was reduced to awed silence by the time they'd gotten to the group from King.

"Mr. Brown says that there are more than a hundred scientists working here under Dr. Church," Janice continued. "More than any other biology lab in the country!"

"It's incredible," Charlie mumbled. He'd never been

great at talking to girls, other than Crystal. He didn't know why, but whenever he was face-to-face with a girl, he felt like he'd just stuck his tongue in a jar of Elmer's Glue.

Thankfully, Crystal broke into the conversation.

"Do you really collect fossils, like that Neanderthal said?"

"I do. Actually, it's pretty much all I do, when I'm not keeping Rod out of trouble. I've got so many that I wrote a paper about them for the state science fair, and then the Museum of Science let me bring them in for a temporary exhibit."

Crystal seemed genuinely impressed. Fossils weren't the same as rocks, but they were closely related. No doubt the two of them had a lot in common.

"Are you here with one of your fossils?" Crystal asked.

"No, I like to identify the fossils myself. That's part of the fun. We're here with something we found in the parking lot of our school, buried right next to Mr. Brown's parking spot."

Mr. Brown was the teacher speaking to Mrs. Hennigan around the corner. Charlie wondered if Mr. Brown also had a personal connection to Dr. Church— though maybe "personal connection" was a bit of an exaggeration to describe the twist of good luck that had put their quirky science teacher in the same orbit as the world-renowned biologist.

Mrs. Hennigan had met Dr. George Church quite by accident, on the subway, of all places. Mrs. Hennigan had told them the story on the elevator ride up from the security booth on the first floor of the New Research Building; the story had been short enough to be told during the thirty-foot vertical rise.

Apparently, Mrs. Hennigan had been taking the T from Copley Square, where she'd gone shopping for tennis sneakers, to Kenmore, where she was supposed to meet a friend for coffee. Along the short trip, she'd noticed a very tall man with a white beard sprawled out on the bench across from her, fast asleep. She'd recognized Dr. Church from television; he'd appeared on plenty of late-night programs talking about everything from climate change to genetic engineering, and Mrs. Hennigan, being a fan of science, qualified as a card-carrying Dr. Church groupie.

As a Dr. Church fan, Mrs. Hennigan knew another important thing about the scientist that the other riders on the subway probably did not: Dr. Church suffered from narcolepsy, a disorder that causes people to fall asleep whenever they sit still, sometimes right in the middle of a sentence. Although "suffered" might not have been the right word: Dr. Church had often said that he sometimes saw his narcolepsy as a gift, because it gave him the ability to sleep at a moment's notice. Airplane flights went by in the blink of an eye, and he never had trouble at night because morning was always just one flitter of his eyelids away.

But falling asleep on the subway between stops was different, and when Mrs. Hennigan woke the tall man from his slumber, saving him from a journey to the very end of the Green Line, wherever that might be, Dr. Church had been thankful enough to give her his e-mail.

"What about you guys?" Janice asked. "What did you bring in to study? Animal, vegetable, or mineral?"

"We're not really sure," Marion butted in from behind Crystal. He wasn't much better with girls than Charlie, but at least he could still speak in complete sentences. "We think it might be some sort of bone."

Janice seemed to light up at the statement, but before she could say more, there was motion from behind her—and a moment later Mrs. Hennigan and Mr. Brown came around the corner, followed by the man Charlie recognized from the newspaper picture Mrs. Hennigan had shown them in her classroom.

At six foot five, Dr. George Church was like an amiable, smiling tree rising up above the two sixth-grade teachers. His white beard took up the lower half of his face, matching his thick shock of silver hair, a chaotic coif of windblown tresses that made it look like the man had just stepped out of a wind tunnel.

Dr. Church had a commanding presence, not just because of his height and his beard and his hair, but because of his accomplishments. He'd been written up in *Time* magazine as one of the most important scientists alive, and he was a pioneer in the science of genetics—the study of DNA, the chemical at the center of all living creatures, often called the building blocks of life. Dr. Church's work was helping doctors find cures for thousands of diseases, and the science going on in his lab could one day be responsible for discovering everything from the cure to cancer to extending life spans.

Even Rod seemed mesmerized by Dr. Church's presence. He quickly joined the rest of the kids—both Charlie's group and the other three from the King School—by a low counter where the scientist carefully laid out two objects in matching metal trays.

Charlie recognized the yellow-white, bonelike specimen he and his friends had found in the Public Garden in one of the trays. The other object was slightly larger than their find, and also white. But it was thinner—almost the narrowness of a pencil—and gnarled at one end.

"So, kids," Dr. Church said, his voice a kind baritone. "I see we have two samples of mysterious materials you both found outside. Let's start with the object from the King School."

Janice wheeled herself toward the counter, obviously speaking for her group.

"We found this in the parking lot. We cleaned it off, and tried to look at it under a microscope. From some gross observation—pardon the pun—we think it's some sort of bone."

Charlie raised his eyebrows, trying to get a better look at the other kids' find. From a distance, it did look like bone—maybe even more so than the object he and his friends had found.

Dr. Church stepped closer to the two trays, squinting from behind a pair of wire-rimmed glasses.

"Interesting," he said. "And the other sample?"

Crystal raised her hand, but when nobody called on her, she simply blurted out her response.

"We found ours partially buried in the Public Garden, and we think it's bone too! We looked at it under a stereomicroscope, but we can't get any deeper than that with what we've got in our lab."

Church grinned.

"That's something I can definitely help you with. In our lab, we can do more than look at the two objects; I think we can figure out what they are—and even how old they are."

"How do we do that?" asked Charlie. "Is it something we can do today?"

Dr. Church reached into a drawer and pulled out a pair of blue plastic gloves. He put the gloves on, then carefully held up the two objects as if he were about to conduct a symphony with them.

"There are many ways to find information like this, but the definitive way is with a process called 'carbon dating.' Basically, it's a way of measuring how old biological material is by measuring the amount of a specific biological chemical, carbon-14, still remaining in them."

Charlie had to think it over several times, running the idea through his brain over and over again before he thought he understood. Basically, living things had a chemical called carbon inside them, and over time, that carbon went away. If you measured how much of that particular form of carbon remained, you could estimate how old something was.

"'Biological material'?" Rod said. "So you do think both of these samples are from living creatures?"

Dr. Church placed the samples back down on the bench in front of him. The kids watched his every move. He moved closer to a large machine with knobs and cranks and a keypad as big as a notebook. He tapped his long fingers on the top of the hunk of metal.

"That's our working hypothesis," he said. "This machine will tell us for sure. Once a plant or animal dies, it stops exchanging the element carbon with its environment. This machine is called an Accelerator Mass Spectrometer."

"Sounds like something that Lex Luthor would have dreamed up to kill Superman," Jeremy said.

Dr. Church laughed.

"Maybe, but it wouldn't kill Superman; it would just tell you how old he is."

He placed his hand on top of a round cylinder on the side of the machine.

"This is the ionizing chamber," he said. "After the sample passes through and gets ionized, it goes through an accelerator, which is right here."

He pointed to yet another cylinder that was housed in a metal box. Connected to that was a smaller cylinder that had orange tubing coming out the side.

"What's that bendy portion?" Kentaro asked.

"There's an electromagnet inside, which deflects

and filters the decaying element and helps us measure how long the specimen has been aging."

"And that will tell us how old it is!" Kentaro shouted.

Dr. Church nearly jumped out of his shoes at Kentaro's enthusiasm, but then something caught his attention. Charlie realized that Dr. Church had suddenly paused, and was now hovering right over their sample, still sitting in its tray.

"Hold on a second," he said.

He reached down to the counter and found a pair of metal tweezers, taking them between two gloved fingers. Carefully, he went to work on their sample, and a few seconds later he rose back up, holding something between the tweezers' blades.

Charlie could barely make out something thin, like a filament or a hair, swaying in the slight breeze from the lab's ventilation system.

"What is it?" Marion said. "Is it something scary?"

Church didn't answer. He seemed almost in an absentminded haze as he turned and headed toward a small microscope standing in a corner by a pair of pewter sinks. Charlie recognized the scientist's state of mind—his parents disappeared into the very same haze multiple times a day, whenever something interesting piqued their scientific minds. Obviously, Church had found something intriguing enough to make him forget he was in his lab in front of a room full of children. For that brief moment, he was in another place, deep in a trance of discovery.

He placed the tiny filament under the microscope, looked for a moment, then sat straight up, suddenly seeing the kids and their teachers, as if for the first time.

"This is pretty cool. And very strange."

Charlie couldn't help himself.

"What is it, Dr. Church? It looks like you found a hair."

Church shook his head. He moved quickly to a pair of cabinets above the sinks and withdrew an iPad, then began pressing at the screen.

"Not a hair. . . . A feather."

And then he turned the iPad to show them a page he'd pulled up from the Internet.

"I've always had an interest in zoology," the scientist said. "And I've gotten pretty good at identifying even the most obscure creatures. But this one is very, very unusual."

The picture on the iPad was of a bird, but not like any bird Charlie had ever seen before. The creature on the screen was huge, immense, with a long, cruel-looking hooked beak and wings as big as a small car. It looked . . . prehistoric.

"Our object is from a bird?" Jeremy whispered, clearly as shocked by the picture as Charlie.

"I don't know about the object yet," Dr. Church said. "The piece of feather seems to have become attached after the fact. I don't think it's necessarily related to the object. But the feather itself—yes, that's from a bird."

He pointed to the fierce-looking creature on the iPad.

"Vultur gryphus," he said.

Charlie stared at him. Then he looked at his friends. They were also staring in silence, until Kentaro piped up:

"An Andean condor. The second-largest wingspan in the world, after the wandering albatross. They are carrion feeders—they eat dead animals. They can grow to ten feet in wingspan. But they live in the Andes Mountains, in South America."

Dr. Church smiled, and the moment felt somehow magical to Charlie—being part of a real-life scientific mystery.

"Why would the feather of a giant bird that lives on the other side of the world be attached to an object we found in the Public Garden?" he asked.

Dr. Church winked at Charlie.

"That's something I can't answer," he said. "But I'm pretty sure I know where you and your friends might go to try to figure it out."

As the great scientist turned back to the two samples, and the sci-fi-looking carbon-dating machine, Charlie's mind whirled forward. He had no idea what sort of adventure they had stumbled into, but he had a feeling it was something much bigger than a piece of old bone unearthed from a pile of dirt.

"I THINK WE'RE IN the right place."

Marion was breathing hard, but it was difficult to tell if it was because he, Charlie, and Jeremy had spent the past forty minutes hiking their way across the Franklin Park Zoo—one of the largest open spaces in the entire city of Boston, and also one of the oldest functioning zoos in the country—or because they'd just stepped into an even more ancient-looking building that stunk of birds, bird food, bird droppings, and just about anything else that had to do with birds.

"I gotta say," Jeremy said, as Marion bent over at the waist, sucking in the fetid air, "this place is pretty darn creepy."

Jeremy wasn't sweating as much as Marion, but

he looked even more disheveled in his Boy Scout uniform, which appeared to be missing at least a quarter of the regulation items. He had on army green pants and shirt, with the requisite badges on his shoulder and the pocket, but he'd exchanged the cloth belt and metal buckle with something that looked like plastic. The telltale scarf around his neck was tied together at his throat; obviously he'd lost the metal clasp. And his hat looked two sizes too big, hanging down almost to his reddish eyebrows. No doubt he'd lost his own hat a long time ago, and had borrowed someone else's.

The fact that Jeremy was still a member of the Scouts was surprising to Charlie; he'd have thought his awkward best friend would have washed out of the group somewhere between Cub Scout and Webelo. It wasn't just the clothes; Jeremy wasn't good with authority, and never had been. He was smart enough to keep out of trouble at school, but he almost never completed homework as it was assigned, and he had a real problem with anything that involved instructions. And from what Charlie had gathered following Jeremy's progress through the organization over the years, the Scouts were all about following the rules.

Then again, Jeremy's dad was a manager at a local supermarket chain, and before that had served in the

U.S. Army; so maybe Jeremy's genetics were helping him navigate his way through. Dr. Church might have been able to shed some light on the subject; maybe Charlie would ask him if Jeremy's nurture had trumped his nature, later on, when they all gathered back at the Church Lab to see the results of the carbon dating.

In the meantime, Charlie had found that Jeremy's Scouts' affiliation lent them the perfect avenue to the next step in their investigation.

"It couldn't have been a tuft of hair from a giraffe?" Jeremy continued, as Marion finally caught his breath and they started forward into the dark, cavelike exhibit. "Or even some gorilla dander? Why did it have to be a bird? I hate birds. And I think I really hate Bird's World."

Charlie had to admit the place really did look frightening—even from the outside. Bird's World was obviously a throwback to the park's earliest architecture, consisting of an Asian-themed arboretum with arched windows, terra-cotta slanted roofs, and huge, gatelike doors rising up between wrought iron cockatoo and parrot cages. Once inside, the trio had been thrown into near darkness, and were now moving through a foyer with concrete floors and fading wooden walls.

Growing up, Jeremy had spent many weekends at the zoo. He was very familiar with the giraffes, kept in a wonderful open-air enclosure near the front of the park. He loved the gorillas and their African-themed home, "The Tropical Forest." But over the years, he'd studiously avoided the time warp called Bird's World.

Luckily, Troop 74 of the local Boy Scouts did not share his apprehensions, and Jeremy's group was already ahead of them, making their way through the anachronistic building. Officially, Jeremy was supposed to be taking part in a scavenger hunt through the zoo, keeping track of everything he was seeing in a little notebook he had in his pocket. But Jeremy, Charlie, and Marion were actually there on a scavenger hunt of their own—following the clue Dr. Church had shared with them, to the only place within a hundred miles that made sense.

"I mean," Jeremy said, "it feels like any minute now the darn thing is going to soar down from the rafters and take my head off."

Andean condor, Charlie repeated in his head. Although Kentaro—and Crystal—hadn't been able to convince their parents to let them join Jeremy and his troop to check out the zoo on a school night, Charlie could still hear his wordsmith of a friend explaining to him how the Franklin Park Zoo didn't just have one of the magnificent birds in its possession, but two. Apparently, the condors naturally lived in pairs. That still didn't explain why a feather from such a bird might have ended up on an object buried in the Public Garden, but it was certainly the first place to look.

Which meant—Bird's World. But poking through the dark arboretum, Charlie hadn't yet seen any evidence of the giant creatures, or anything that would explain the object they'd left in Church's lab.

One step at a time, Charlie told himself, as they reached a door leading beneath a carved wooden sign that read WETLANDS. From the dust around the sign, the place looked like it had to be about forty years old, and it also appeared like the "wetlands" hadn't changed much in that amount of time. Once through the door, Charlie found himself in a circular room with an artificial pond taking up most of the back half, complete with a muddy shoreline which ran right up to a waist-high, thick pane of glass. The glass had a few dings but seemed relatively intact, despite the many decades of kids that had surely rubbed their fingers, faces, and god knows what else against the surface.

"It's still pretty dark in here," said Marion. "I can't tell if it's my allergies or my bad vision, but I can't see much past the glass. You guys see any condors?"

Charlie's eyes adjusted pretty fast, but he wasn't expecting condors in the wetlands. He knew the giant birds would be kept outside, in some sort of enclosure at the other end of the building, which they'd be through in a few short minutes. For the moment they were just following the Scouts, because there was no way Charlie's parents would have let him visit the zoo on a Wednesday night on his own.

"I think there's a family of finches on the other side of the glass," he said.

Jeremy was hanging back, so Charlie moved next to Marion, closer to the swampy water, trying to get a better look. He felt a drop of moisture drip from the ceiling above. It was so humid in the wetlands that the room was starting to leak. Charlie was about to step back, to head deeper into the exhibit, when there was a flash of movement, and then a cold, wet splash against his face.

"Joke's on you, Numbers!"

Dylan Wigglesworth crashed into the glass right between Charlie and Marion, a meaty paw scooping up a second handful of water to toss in Charlie's direction. This time Charlie ducked, and the murky, muddy liquid splashed all the way back to where Jeremy was standing, marking his already stained Boy Scout shirt.

"Aw, come on!" Jeremy shouted, but Dylan was already reaching over the glass for another handful of the wetlands to toss at Marion, who was tumbling backward to get away from their oversize classmate.

"Time to get up close and personal with the swamp!" Dylan roared, hitting Marion with a blast of the dank water.

Jeremy was still sputtering in Dylan's direction, something about how Dylan was disgracing his own Boy Scout uniform by soaking a troop mate's, but Charlie knew it was useless; there was no reasoning with his nemesis. Some kids took to bullying because they were insecure or jealous, or had difficult home lives. Dylan Wigglesworth truly enjoyed torturing Charlie and his friends; to Dylan, it was an all-American sport, on par with baseball. Even though Jeremy was also at the zoo on the same Scout trip as Dylan, that didn't endow Charlie's friend with any special treatment.

"Hey, Diapers," Dylan yelled, "how about a merit badge in sludge?"

Now he had both hands in the exhibit, and Charlie knew it was time to attempt an escape, if they wanted to get home with any articles of dry clothing.

Charlie looked around wildly and caught sight of a door set flush with a giant portrait of some sort of waterfowl, right past where the glass of the wetlands exhibit ended. Although the door appeared to be some sort of emergency exit, Charlie doubted any alarms would go off; heck, this building was probably built before Edison invented the lightbulb.

"Dylan!" Charlie shouted, pointing toward a spot in the water, just beyond where the bully's hands were scooping up a really big blob of muddy scum. "Is that a piranha? I'm pretty sure they're native to the wetlands."

Dylan's eyes widened and he jerked back, splashing himself in the process. Then his eyes narrowed as he shook black water from his cheeks.

"There aren't any piranhas in Bird's World—" he started, but Charlie was already racing past him, heading for the door.

Charlie grabbed Marion by the shirt collar and hit the door shoulder first, followed a foot behind by Jeremy. The three of them burst out into a dark hallway, sped through another door—and then into a wooded area right behind the arboretum. The door clanged shut behind them.

"Quickly," Charlie snapped, leading them hard to the right, through a break in the trees to a small path that wound around toward the back of the building. There was no way to know if Dylan would follow them or stick with the rest of the Boy Scout troop. Charlie didn't intend to stay around long enough to find out.

The three of them kept moving, tracing a path by a pair of cages containing macaws—both of which were sleeping, long, colorful beaks tucked beneath their wings. Charlie couldn't blame them; it was already beginning to get dark outside, which meant the zoo would be closing soon. In a few minutes, Dylan or no Dylan, he and his friends would have to double back and meet up with the rest of the Scouts. But Charlie felt fairly certain that the presence of the troop leader would protect them long enough to get them to the parking lot, where their parents would be waiting.

In the meantime, they still had a mission to complete. A few more yards along the path and Charlie finally caught sight of their quarry: a massive steel enclosure that looked like something right out of *Jurassic Park*. The scale of the enclosure was almost incomprehensible, consisting of a huge, curved center atrium and a pair of long, caged catwalks bisecting the middle.

In all of Charlie's visits to the Franklin Park Zoo, he had never been inside the condor cage. As magnificent as it was, it was also terrifying, like something out of a different era, that looked like it had been built to house pterodactyls.

"There they are," Jeremy whispered, pointing through the links in the cage.

Charlie squinted through the darkness—and caught sight of the two birds, standing fairly close to each other beneath a low bush at the center of the enclosure. Even from a distance, they were enormous—really, prehistoric. Though their wings were down, Charlie guessed that outstretched, they had to be as long as Dr. Church was tall. And those beaks—those crazy, supersharp beaks— looked like they could tear a person's arm right off.

Charlie knew the condors were safely trapped in their cage, and that even if they weren't, they were like vultures—they feasted on dead animals, not live ones. But even so, he didn't relish the idea of investigating their habitat further.

"I guess we have to go inside," he said reluctantly— when Marion grabbed his arm.

"Maybe not. Check that out."

Marion was pointing to the left, to a row of bushes right up next to the condor exhibit, flush with the cor- rugated caging that ran up the curved center of the enclosure. There appeared to be a break in the bushes, an opening leading to another area of the park.

"Does that go to another part of Bird's World?" Charlie asked.

Marion shook his head. He'd basically memorized the map of the zoo before they'd come.

"That isn't on the map; it's something new."

Charlie figured it was worth checking out. They

could always turn back and go into the condor cage if there was nothing to see beyond the bushes. He led his two friends in the direction of the condors, carefully picking his way off the path. He sidled along the edge of the cage—keeping a careful side-eye watch on the two birds, which were still thankfully on the other side of the enclosure—to the break in the bushes.

Then they were through the opening, and found themselves facing another fence—this one rising straight up in front of them. Unlike the condor enclosure, this barrier was made up of wooden slats, obscuring their view. But standing on his toes, Charlie managed to reach a small crevasse between two of the slats, pushing his face close to the wood so he could see inside.

"Wow," he murmured.

Spread out in front of him, for as far as he could see, was what appeared to be reddish sand—rising in low dunes, falling into curved valleys—a landscape that looked nothing like the rest of the zoo. Farther on, past one of the dunes, he could make out construction in process: bulldozers parked side by side, large piles of wood, wrapped building frames, and sheets of glass. Whatever the construction site was, it was massive. And beyond the bulldozers, he could just barely make out a dome-shaped structure covered in white tarp.

Jeremy, then Marion, took turns at the crevasse, then the three of them stepped back from the fence, thinking.

"This definitely isn't on the map," Marion said.

He reached into his pocket, illustrating his point by holding up the detailed pamphlet he had printed off the Internet, pointing out the various exhibits—none of which included a massive, dune-covered environment.

Before either Charlie or Jeremy could respond, Marion pulled his pen out of his pocket—the same pen, it appeared, that he had used to dig in the Public Garden—and began marking the map.

"What are you doing?" Jeremy asked. "We don't have time for a portrait. This isn't art class."

Charlie could see Marion's eyebrows furrowing and his nose crinkling up. Marion stayed focused on the map and kept on drawing. Then, he again reached into his pocket and pulled out a tiny, portable measuring tape, and continued to sketch lines across the map, using the tape measure to draw them perfectly straight.

"I think he knows what he's doing," Charlie said, a little uncertainty in his voice.

"Yes, I do. I'm triangulating."

"Sorry?" Jeremy asked. "I think there's a porta-potty on the other side of Bird's World."

"Not urinating," Marion jeered. "Triangulating. Sailors used to use the technique to avoid storms, and seismologists still use the science to track earthquakes."

"That sounds helpful," Jeremy grunted. "If I see a storm or an earthquake, I'll be sure to triangulate my way out of here."

Marion ignored him.

"We know the distance from Bird's World to the condor cage, and we also know the distance from the Tropical Forest exhibit to the condor cage. With these two points of reference, we can deduct exactly where this place should be on the map."

"That's great and all," said Charlie, "but how is finding it on the map going to help us?"

Charlie knew that triangulation was one of the oldest methods used in mapmaking, and had even been employed to measure the size of the earth in 1048. In the sixth century, the Greek philosopher Thales had used triangulation to measure the height of the pyramids.

"Maybe if I figure out where this fits on the map," Marion continued, "we can make an educated guess about what it's supposed to be—"

"Or," Jeremy suddenly said, "we could just read this sign."

He had stepped three feet down along the wooden

fence, and was pointing to a plaque affixed to the top of the slats, which was slightly higher than his head.

The words were written in bold italics: *H. I. African Savanna.*

"Okay," Marion said. "An African savanna. But I still think the triangulation is worthwhile. Once I have the exact specifications of the lot, I can look up the construction permits. All construction of this size has to have permits, and there are databases where this stuff gets filed away."

Charlie continued peering up at the sign. Squinting, he saw more letters, much smaller than the headline: ACTIVE CONSTRUCTION SITE PER ORDERS OF THE CITY OF BOSTON IN CONJUNCTION WITH HEADSTROM INDUSTRIES.

"Headstrom Industries," he said out loud.

He didn't think he'd heard the name before. He didn't know if it was a construction company or some sort of zoo-related entertainment business. All he knew was that Franklin Park Zoo was obviously getting a new exhibit—something huge, right next to the condor cage. Close enough that an errant feather might very well have floated over the pickets of that tall, wooden fence. . . .

"I like the color of the sand," Jeremy mused. "Red. It's also the best color for hair."

"I don't disagree," Marion said.

Charlie had often wondered why two of his best friends were similarly ginger. Then he had another thought—the sand certainly didn't look like anything that he'd ever seen in Massachusetts before. He didn't know where it might have come from—but he knew someone who would be able to figure it out.

He bent down and stuck his fingers beneath the base of the wooden fence. Within a few seconds, he found a small sample—really, a few dozen reddish-streaked pebbles –and put them in his pocket.

Then he rose and nodded toward the break in the bushes leading back to Bird's World, Dylan, and the Boy Scout troop.

"I think our time is up," he said. "We'd better head back before we get locked in here overnight with a couple of hungry birds."

"They only eat you when you're dead," Jeremy said.

"Somehow," Marion replied, "that doesn't make me feel any better."

Charlie smiled, patting his pocket as he followed his friends away from the construction site. They may have been on their way out of the zoo, but they were definitely not leaving a stone unturned.

IT WAS TEN MINUTES past noon the next day, and the lunchroom at Nagassack Middle was bustling. The barely choreographed chaos of eighty sixth-grade students rushing through the converted gym of a hall to eat their food and, more important, finish as soon as they could so they could fill the rest of the period with playground time, was beyond palpable. In the midst of the chaos, one thing remained constant: The Whiz Kids were at their spot near the back of the vast room, a bastion of calm in the churning sea of hungry classmates, and it was time for their regular lunchtime Meeting of Minds.

Charlie lowered himself onto a green circular stool next to Crystal at the rectangular table. The fragrance of the beans-and-rice concoction on his lunch tray vaguely reminded him of the BBQ restaurants his dad loved to take them to on special occasions. Though his parents were both vegetarians, the side dishes at legendary Boston institutions such as the Smoke Shop and Sweet Cheeks were enough for a perfect family meal. Beans at the school cafeteria were by no means the same quality, but they were far better than the greenish-hued meat loaf that served as the main choice that particular Thursday.

Marion reached the table next, placing his tray down nearly in sync with Jeremy, who was followed by Kentaro. Kentaro was usually the last to reach their spot; his little legs had to work twice as hard to travel the same distance as the rest of them, and the place was big; it had once served as a basketball court, until Nagassack ran into financial issues that had led to the school dropping a handful of less popular sports. The foul line and shooting box still remained, faded blue lines marking the wood floor where the teachers' table now sat; but no matter how many teachers crowded around their industrial-looking perch, they almost never got involved in the day-to-day mob scene of kids that surrounded them.

Once all the Whiz Kids were gathered, Jeremy

moved his tray of beans and rice to the side to make room for his backpack on the shiny faux-wood table. Then he reached inside and, with a flourish, retrieved the sample of reddish pebbles that Charlie had recovered from the zoo.

"Close your eyes," he said to Crystal, "and put out your hand."

Crystal looked from him to Charlie, who nodded. Charlie had given the sample to Jeremy to hold on to, because Jeremy almost always had his backpack with him. Even after the darn thing had gifted him with the worst nickname in middle school history, he still held on to it, like a security blanket.

Crystal shrugged, then played along and closed her eyes and reached out her hand. Jeremy plopped the reddish pebbles into her palm.

Crystal opened her eyes and peered down at the sample, dwelling on the interesting concentric-circle patterns on the stones, which alternated between rough and smooth surfaces. Then Crystal turned her head to speak to Charlie.

"You want me to make myself a new necklace? The red color is pretty, but I don't think these would qualify as gemstones."

Charlie pulled Marion's crumpled map of the

Franklin Park Zoo, still covered in his triangulation marks, from his pocket.

"If you like African jewelry, it might be perfect," he said.

Crystal took the map from his hands, then looked at the reddish pebbles again, even more intrigued.

Most of the girls in the sixth-grade class at Nagassack stuck together and had no interest in rocks—and definitely no interest in any of the Whiz Kids. But the opposite was true of Crystal. She could take the most minute sample, of the darkest rock, and find it remarkable. To top it off, she could take that same sample and fashion it into something even more beautiful. She loved identifying each rock and adding it to her rock collection, then polishing it and turning it into jewelry. Mrs. Hennigan had even once asked her if she wanted to start selling her jewelry at the school fair. But that didn't interest Crystal. Her collection was dear to her, a part of her history, and a part of what made her fascinating to the Whiz Kids, to Charlie especially.

Charlie and Crystal had been friends since second grade, and Charlie had always thought of her as more like a sister than anything else. But he had to admit, sometimes, now that they were older, things felt a little different.

He chided himself, realizing it was probably just the excitement of seeing Crystal so happy to have a new sample to identify. Then he quickly pushed his feelings aside as Kentaro touched his shoulder, pointing to Mrs. Hennigan, who was heading toward them.

Mrs. Hennigan had a determined pace to her gait, her white curls bouncing with each step. Charlie could see a teal South Beach Diet–branded box with a picture of a chicken dinner on the front in her hand—another odd characteristic of their science teacher: She was always eating prepared meals. Not because she needed to diet—she had never been plump as long as they'd known her—but because she loved the preciseness of measured-out meals.

When she reached their table, she gave them a beaming smile, her teeth almost as white as Mabel's toes.

"Good news, kids! Dr. Church just e-mailed me; the lab results are in!"

Charlie felt a thrill move through him.

"Was it really bone?" he asked. "And was it old?"

Mrs. Hennigan shook her head.

"We'll have to find out together. You're all going to miss fourth period today. Call it a scientific field trip."

Then she glanced down at the table, to the reddish pebbles in Crystal's hands.

"Though it looks like some of you might have already been on a field trip since we last spoke."

She seemed to be about to ask something else—then instead smiled, and held her box of frozen chicken above their heads.

"We'll talk more this afternoon. I've got exactly thirteen point seven ounces of fowl to microwave before the next bell."

And then she was off, and Charlie was watching Crystal toss the reddish pebbles in the air, catching them with a little wink in his direction. He could feel the slightest hint of butterflies rise up again in his stomach, which he quickly chased away. Then he took another bite of his beans.

CHARLIE STOOD NEXT TO the wooden security desk, nervously tapping his feet, as one by one Crystal, Marion, Kentaro, then Jeremy bumped into him like bowling pins about to go down after being hit by a ball. If gracefulness were quantifiable, the Whiz kids, especially when they were overeager, would have broken records for the lowest possible scores.

It was midafternoon by the time they arrived at the New Research Building and found their way to the security desk, which was staffed by a guard in an official-looking uniform. The guy had a clipboard and a goatee, and Charlie wasn't sure which was more intimidating. On their previous visit to the Harvard building, they'd been led by Mrs. Hennigan, but this time around

Mrs. Hennigan had gone on ahead, leaving them to be dropped off at the building's front lobby by one of the other science teachers, Mr. Kraft, a quiet man in his midfifties who hadn't asked any questions and hadn't wanted any answers.

Charlie watched as the goatee took down their names and cross-referenced them with the sheet of paper on the top of the clipboard.

Then they were past the desk and on their way to the meccalike labs of the second floor.

The guts of the building were just as impressive as the exterior; the building itself was a glass rectangle that looked kind of like a large Lego fortress. The elevators were likewise cubic and shiny, and opened onto a nicely carpeted foyer. But after that, it was all a maze. If Charlie hadn't been there before, and didn't have Marion with him—a master of charts and maps—they would never have found the Church Lab.

But once they'd gotten their bearings, it was a short walk to a familiar area of the lab they'd been to before— and Charlie immediately caught sight of the great scientist, pacing back and forth, talking animatedly to one of his postdoctorate students, a man with a name tag on his white jacket that read BOBBY.

From a distance, Charlie overheard Dr. Church

saying something about a recent order of synthetic pig DNA. Bobby was tall and Indian and was waving a tiny Ziploc bag in the air, saying something about it being incomplete. To Bobby, a bag of synthetic DNA must have been something he saw every day, something common, but to Charlie, it was simply amazing.

Charlie knew from his own scientific research that DNA was the basic chemical building block of life. Every cell in the human body—in all living creatures— had DNA in it. Synthetic DNA, on the other hand, was DNA that was made in a laboratory.

Charlie couldn't believe the postdoc was holding an actual bag of synthetic DNA so nonchalantly. It was one thing to order pig parts—Charlie knew that transplant surgeons even used pig livers in experiments—but to actually order DNA, made from scratch, seemed like science fiction.

Then Dr. Church saw Charlie and his friends, and quickly waved them over. Moving deeper into the lab, Charlie saw that Mrs. Hennigan was already tucked into the far corner of the room, next to a bench with a dozen pipettes and test tubes scattered all around. Next to her, he also saw Janice, as well as the rest of her crew from the King School. Janice waved at him, Rod glared at him, and the other two kids ignored him; but

Charlie was too caught up in the energy of the lab to really notice any of them.

The place was hopping, much more active than when they'd last been there, probably because it was now a workday, and everything seemed to be both frenzied and controlled at the same time. Kind of like a synchronized ballet: One student in a white lab coat dodging the next, who was whisking a clear DNA gel away to read under a microscope, while a third student, wearing thick gloves, was reaching into a liquid-nitrogen vat of frozen samples. Smoke, smoke, smoke, and more smoke. So much smoke—the same kind Charlie had seen in plays back at Nagassack, as the gloved student grabbed a metal box from the icy chamber, bringing up another sample of frozen DNA.

As the sizzle of liquid nitrogen diminished, Dr. Church turned to the group of kids, and a big smile spread across his bearded face. As he moved toward them, Charlie caught sight of a woman standing a few feet away, watching; the woman was Asian, short and compact, and looked extremely young—maybe too young to be a postdoc or even a medical student. She was holding a notebook and seemed to be taking notes. She wasn't wearing a lab coat, but instead had on a pair of navy slacks and a white button-down blouse. Plenty of the students seemed to be in plainclothes too, so her outfit didn't mean anything. Still, Charlie wondered who she might be. Maybe a daughter of one of the professors?

Church didn't seem bothered by her presence, so Charlie figured she was supposed to be there. He turned his attention back to the scientist, who stopped three feet short of the group and pulled a folded sheet of paper from the pocket of his lab coat.

"I have some good news, and some slightly less interesting news. One of the samples your two groups brought me is something really groundbreaking and important, and the other is, well—not. Before I give you my results, let's talk hypotheses."

Janice rolled her chair an inch closer, as if she were trying to get a glimpse of Church's paper.

"We both think our samples are some sort of bone."

"A good assumption," Church replied. "And one of the samples is indeed bone. The other is related to bone. Similar to bone, but denser, with no internal blood-vessel system."

Charlie's thoughts raced in his head. *Similar, but denser. No blood-vessel system.*

"A tooth?" he said out loud.

Laughter erupted from the other kids. Charlie felt his cheeks turning red.

"A tooth?" Rod said. "Both samples are more than nine inches long. You think Jaws was hanging out in the Public Garden?"

"Ah," Dr. Church interrupted, raising a hand. "But Charlie is on the right track."

"What?" Kentaro blurted. "One of these samples is a tooth?"

"Not a tooth. A tusk."

The room went silent.

"A tusk?" Jeremy said. "Like an elephant?"

Church turned and pointed toward the machine he had shown them on their last visit.

"Like an elephant—but not an elephant. We compared the carbon-decay rate and calculated the age of the tusk fragment. And we came to the conclusion that the tusk one of you found is actually more than twenty thousand years old."

Charlie gasped, but the noise was lost because everyone in the room was gasping at once. Even Mrs. Hennigan had turned pale, her eyes wide like manhole covers. Staring at Dr. Church, Charlie also caught sight of the young Asian woman, who had moved closer while the great scientist had been speaking. Obviously, she had overheard what Church had said, because her eyes had also gone wide with surprise.

"Twenty thousand years old," Charlie murmured. "So this tusk is from—"

"A woolly mammoth," Janice whispered. As an expert in fossils and things prehistoric, she had no doubt made the jump even before Charlie.

"A woolly mammoth?" repeated Jeremy. "Like in the movie *Jurassic Park*?"

"There are no woolly mammoths in *Jurassic Park*," Janice corrected. "Woolly mammoths weren't around when dinosaurs roamed the Earth. Dinosaurs lived sixty-five million years ago. Mammoths are from the last ice age, which ended about ten thousand years ago. The mammoth is an ancestor to modern elephants. Huge creatures often covered in reddish hair."

"Like Tweedledee and Tweedledum," Rod said, pointing to Jeremy and Marion.

"Maybe, but mammoths could live in temperatures as low as what's in that nitrogen freezer."

"That's correct," Dr. Church said, pleased. "They were happiest at minus seventy degrees Fahrenheit. In fact, that freezer contains samples of woolly meat, from which we've been harvesting DNA."

"The Woolly Mammoth Revival Project," Charlie said.

He'd read about the Woolly Mammoth Revival

Project in the newspaper a few times, and had even discussed it with his parents at a number of dinners. Over the past four years, Dr. Church had put together a team of scientists in an effort to bring back the prehistoric creature by synthesizing the animal's DNA from frozen samples brought back from the Arctic Circle. The goal was to use that DNA to essentially grow a woolly mammoth in a laboratory. It sounded like science fiction, but as one of Dr. Church's students liked to say, it was only science fiction until you took the fiction away. Then it was just science.

"So you're saying that one of our samples is part of a woolly mammoth tusk?" asked Jeremy, bewildered. "Could a woolly mammoth have once lived in Boston?"

"A cousin of the mammoth—the mastodon—lived as far south as the continental United States, but woolly mammoths were mostly confined to the tundra of the Arctic."

If that was true, Charlie wondered, how could either of the groups have found a woolly tusk in Massachusetts? He slowly raised his hand. Dr. Church pointed in his direction, signaling for him to proceed.

"It just seems impossible that a tusk that old, from a creature not native to these parts, could have naturally found its way to the Public Garden."

"By the same logic," Janice interjected, "I can't imagine that a woolly mammoth tusk would have been found in the King School parking lot, either."

Church shrugged.

"Both of your conclusions are sound, but the tusk was indeed found in one of those locations: the Public Garden. It appears that Mrs. Hennigan's students have made an amazing discovery. And our friends from the King School found something a little closer to home: a steak bone, probably from a porterhouse. I'm a vegetarian, so I can't say for sure, but I'm guessing whoever dropped it in the parking lot had just enjoyed a wonderful meal."

Janice seemed let down, but next to her, Rod looked like he was about to punch someone. To Charlie, it was no big deal that their sample was the important one. But Rod seemed like he had something more to prove. Even though he had endured many encounters with bullies, Charlie had never figured out how a bully's mind worked, or why with bullies everything had to turn into a competition. Maybe it had something to do with their obsession with team sports? Charlie had never successfully hit or caught a ball in his entire life.

To Charlie, it was more important to understand the science of what the material was, and it didn't matter where the sample had been found. Charlie was happy to have help if Janice and her friends wanted to come along.

Heck, he and his Whiz Kids needed all the help they could get. Church had just told them that they had found a twenty-thousand-year-old fragment of a woolly mammoth tusk in the middle of Boston's Public Garden. Now that they knew what their sample was, the question had become—how did it get there?

And why?

CHARLIE'S FAMILY MINIVAN PULLED up to the bright yellow, vinyl-sided house wedged in between two identical cookie-cutter homes at the top of a windy road bisecting the Mission Hill neighborhood of Boston. Almost before Charlie's mom tapped her horn, Charlie saw the screen door pop open, and watched as Janice began to maneuver her chair out onto the ramp leading down from her front porch.

Charlie instinctively moved to jump out of the minivan to help—when he saw a flash of dark hair and olive skin behind Janice: Rod was there, coming out of her house behind her, and was already helping by holding open the door with one hand, guiding her chair with the other.

What is he doing here, in Janice's house? Charlie knew they were classmates, and maybe even friends, but the way they were interacting, smiling and laughing as they went down the ramp, made Charlie wonder if there was something more going on.

The closest Charlie had ever come to having a girl-friend himself was a deep friendship he'd developed with a girl named Kelly Greene, a student at the Worth Hooks School in New Haven, Connecticut. They had gotten to know each other over the course of a much different adventure—involving a paper airplane contest and some missing moon rocks, which had led Charlie and his Whiz Kids all the way to the National Air and Space Museum in Washington, DC. He and Kelly had worked together to solve that mystery, and had ended up kissing each other on the cheek.

It seemed like a lot to Charlie at the time, but then again, he wasn't exactly socially advanced. He rarely talked to girls, unless he counted Crystal, and he hardly ever counted Crystal.

It had taken a fair amount of nerve for Charlie to invite Janice on that Sunday morning's mission back to the Public Garden, to go deeper into the mystery of the woolly mammoth tusk. He felt certain that she could be a lot of help; her knowledge of fossils and the prehistoric world made her a valuable asset in a mystery involving a mammoth.

Crystal, who was now seated in the second row of the minivan, next to Kentaro, had seemed wary of the idea of bringing a veritable stranger along. But Charlie was sure Crystal and Janice would eventually become fast friends; how could a geology expert and a fossil collector not find something in common?

But when Charlie had invited Janice, he hadn't expected the invitation to include Rod as well. And neither did the rest of the Whiz Kids.

"Great, this should be fun," Marion deadpanned from the third row of seats, where he was sprawled out next to Jeremy's elongated body.

Jeremy guffawed, but Charlie ignored them. Janice was down the ramp and moving along the short path that led to where Charlie's mom had parked. Rod was walking next to her, a hand on top of her chair.

When they arrived at the car, Rod leaned down and picked Janice up in his arms, as Kentaro made room for the petite girl next to him in the second row. Then Rod rolled the chair to the back of the minivan and, with Charlie's mother's help, loaded it in.

Then Rod was back at the side door. Janice's light blue dress covered the seat around her, and Rod helped move it over so that he could climb past and into the third row, next to Jeremy. With Marion beside them, it was like a clown car in the back of the van, but Charlie tried not to smile. He could see the miserable looks on both Marion's and Jeremy's face.

As they pulled away from the curb, the van went silent, save for the tinny sound of Christmas music pumping through the car's speakers. Even though it was more than eight weeks past Christmas, Charlie's mom always played Christmas music in the car when she drove. She believed it kept the car calm, but Charlie was always embarrassed when anyone he didn't know joined them for a drive.

"Is this 'Rudolph the Red-Nosed Reindeer'?" Rod asked. "Interesting choice of music, Mrs. Lewis. Wasn't Christmas a couple of months ago?"

"Charlie's mom likes to keep the joy flowing deep into August," Jeremy said.

Charlie turned to look daggers at his gangly friend, but Rod just smiled, not unkindly.

"What a fine idea, Mrs. Lewis. And thanks again for picking us up. My mother works on weekends, or she would have taken us herself."

Charlie glanced at Crystal, who seemed to be thinking the same thing. Was this the same Rod who had nearly raised a fist at them at Dr. Church's lab just a few days ago? Rod was obviously laying it on thick because there was an adult in the car. Janice had gone quiet; although she'd been talkative at the lab, she now seemed shy. Maybe being in the car with so many people was intimidating, or maybe she was letting Rod do the talking for her.

By the time the minivan had reached the corner of Charles and Beacon Streets and the entrance to the Public Garden, "Little Drummer Boy" was playing on the radio, and Rod had told them all about his family—how he lived with his single mother right next door to Janice, and how they considered themselves cousins, since they'd known each other since kindergarten. How his mom worked really long hours as head of security at a municipal building downtown, and he was pretty much on his own most of the time. How he wanted to be a football player when he grew up, or maybe a boxer. And how it was Janice's fault that he'd ended up at Dr. Church's lab; on his own, he didn't know the difference between a test tube and a tesla.

As Charlie's mom double-parked by the entrance to the park and hit the button to open the back hatch, Charlie had to admit: The kid could be pretty charming when he wanted to be. It was slightly unnerving, how he had gone from violent bully to perfect gentleman, but Charlie figured that if Janice was willing to put up with him, he couldn't be all bad.

The kids quickly unloaded from the van and recovered Janice's chair. Then Charlie said good-bye to his mother, who would run some errands then pick them up in a couple of hours. Until then, they were on their own.

It took less than ten minutes for the group to make their way past the Make Way for Ducklings statues, then around the bridge where the Swan Boats rested, to the corner of the park where they had been digging a week earlier.

Although a fair amount of time had passed, they could still see the remains of Marion's excavation: the small pile of dirt on one side, the depression he had dug with his pen, the stamped-down snow, mud, and leaves where they had all been gathered when they'd found the tusk.

As they approached, Crystal suddenly took charge.

"Kentaro, you, Rod, and Marion line up on the far side of the hole. Janice, you, Jeremy, and Charlie line up over here. We need to comb over this place like it's a crime scene."

Rod sneered, a stark change to the parent-friendly visage he had been wearing through the entire car ride from Mission Hill.

"Oh boy, *CSI*, kindergarten style. Who died and made you class monitor?"

Crystal ignored him.

"Stay close to the ground. We don't want to miss anything. We'll start at the dig site, then move backward, inch by inch."

As everyone went down to their knees, Charlie took the opportunity to sidle up next to Janice's chair, out of earshot from the rest of the group.

"I don't know if we're going to find anything out here, but I'm glad you decided to join us," he said, awkwardly. He wanted to say more, but he couldn't quite find the words.

"How could I resist? A woolly mammoth tusk? Just thinking about it blows my mind. And, anyway, you gave me and Rod something to do on the weekend besides play video games."

"So you and Rod are pretty close?"

"When his dad passed away, he didn't have anyone to lean on—and I was there, right next door. I kind of became a shoulder for him, you know, to rest his head on when things got too sad. I know he can be a jerk, but we take care of each other."

Charlie suddenly felt bad for some of the thoughts he'd had about Rod. Sure, the kid had treated him poorly—but you never knew what other people were dealing with. It didn't excuse his being a bully, but Rod deserved some sympathy.

"As you can see," Janice said, nodding toward her legs, "both Rod and I have lost something—although I don't even think of it that way anymore. I know I'm different, but we're all different, right? We've gotten here walking—or rolling—along different roads, but we're all here now, aren't we?"

Charlie looked at Janice's brown eyes. So much honesty, so much calm, so much strength. The noise of the Public Garden seemed like a distant whir. He didn't quite know what to say.

"It's okay," Janice said. "I know myself. And Rod gets on my nerves, sure, but he feels better when he's by my side, so I let it slide. And plus, it's nice to have a buddy around—even if he can be a brute."

"I think 'brute' is an understatement," Charlie said, pointing.

Although Crystal still had half the group working her *CSI* crime scene, Rod had carried Kentaro up a short grass hill beneath a pair of weeping willow trees and was now rolling the little linguist down the slope, like a log. Kentaro's tiny body was kicking up dirt and grass as Rod howled with laughter.

"Rod!" Janice yelled. "Leave him alone!"

Rod looked up, then jammed his hands into his pockets and feigned innocence.

"Just making sure we don't miss any evidence. I figured one of us needed to get up close and personal with the ground."

Kentaro rose to his feet and brushed grass off his pants.

"I think every inch was fully covered," he said. Then he looked down toward his neon red sneakers. "You scuffed my sneakers. These things are collector's items—"

"Kentaro, don't move," Crystal shouted.

Charlie followed Crystal's eyes. Right in front of where Kentaro was standing, he saw it: a perfectly formed footprint preserved in a patch of frozen mud. It definitely wasn't Kentaro's—it was much bigger than his neon shoes. In fact, it was bigger than any of their shoes—even Rod's. It had to be an adult shoe, size ten or more. And even from a distance, Charlie could tell it wasn't a sneaker—the tread marks were deep and patterned, like some sort of work boot.

Janice pointed past where Kentaro was standing, to another print a few steps behind him.

"There are more. You think these could be from a week ago?"

"It's been cold enough," Charlie said. "And they seem to lead right up to where we found the tusk. But it's hard to know for sure."

Crystal reached into her pocket and pulled out a Ziploc bag filled with powder. She beckoned to Jeremy, pointing to the water bottle in the side pocket of his ever-present backpack.

As the rest of the group watched, she carefully poured half the bottle into the plastic bag, then resealed it, using her hands to knead the plastic. A minute later she unzipped the top corner of the bag, knelt down low over the first frozen footprint they had found, and poured the sour-cream-like contents out into the print. Then she took a nearby stick and patted the viscous white liquid into the corners.

"Now's not the time to make mud pies," Rod said.

Crystal didn't look up from her work.

"Thanks to your shenanigans, we might just have found a clue. And this is not a mud pie. This is an exothermic reaction—a combination of chemicals that together, when infused with water, can reach temperatures high enough to form large crystals. The crystals will interlock, harden, and turn into a plaster mold."

Rod stared at Crystal, shocked. Janice shook her head, her braids bouncing with the motion.

"Seriously. Who carries powdered plaster with them in their pocket? You're Batman, girl."

Crystal laughed, but Rod was still trying to digest what was going on in front of him.

"It's just a footprint," he said.

"Maybe," Charlie responded, watching Crystal with a mixture of pride and anticipation. "But it might also be evidence."

A woolly mammoth tusk, a condor feather, and a footprint. Three bits of evidence that should have had nothing to do with one another—and yet all of them were somehow tied to that corner of the Public Garden.

It was up to him, his Whiz Kids, and his new companions to figure out how.

THE NEXT AFTERNOON, FIVE minutes after the
final bell, Charlie, Jeremy, Marion, Kentaro, and Crystal
crowded together at a table just a few feet away from
Mabel's hanging skeletal toes. Crystal's steady hand
worked a fine-haired brush over the alabaster mold
she'd made of the frozen footprint. Returning to Mrs.
Hennigan's lab to continue their investigation had been
a no-brainer; now that Mrs. Hennigan knew what they
were up to, she had happily left them alone at their
work. This was, after all, science—and to her, there
was nothing more sacred. The only difficulty had been
waiting until the end of the school day. All five of them
had told their parents that they needed to stay after
for an extracurricular, though none of them had been

particularly explicit about what sort of extracurricular it was. For the moment they still didn't want to involve their parents—for the simple reason that a woolly mammoth tusk was something so valuable, there was a good chance a parent would have thought that such an object should have gone straight to some sort of authority, maybe even a museum.

And maybe they would have been right; after all, according to the research Charlie had done on the Internet after he'd gotten home from the Public Garden the night before, woolly mammoth tusks were insanely valuable. A single full tusk could be worth upward of two hundred and fifty thousand dollars. And though what they had found was much smaller than a full tusk—really no more than a fragment—it was still worth a lot. And mammoth ivory was perfectly legal—unlike elephant ivory, which came from endangered elephants and had led to the killing of thousands of elephants by poachers. Mammoth ivory was being harvested every day by explorers in the Arctic tundra and was still rare enough to make its way into museums and jewelry stores.

But Charlie also knew that if a parent had turned the fragment of tusk over to an authority, or a museum, that would be the end of the mystery—because it was doubtful to him that anyone else would have been obsessed enough to have continued investigating a fragment of tusk as thoroughly as the Whiz Kids. Most people could let something like that go—but not Charlie, and not his friends. This is what they lived for.

Crystal worked carefully over the three-dimensional footprint, using the brush to dust away any errant pieces of dirt and grass that had gotten caught in her pouring process. The fine hairs of the brush swept through every crevice in the plaster, debriding and cleaning. She wasn't just trying to get the thing clean—she was preparing it for computer scanning. Marion had explained that the sample needed to be at least 90 percent free and clear of any contaminants for the computer-modeling software he'd installed on the laptop he'd borrowed from the school AV lab to provide an accurate measurement of the footprint, and Crystal was almost as detail oriented as he was. She was going to get that sample clean enough to eat off of, let alone computer model.

"Whoa," Crystal suddenly said, as the brush stopped in a deep groove near the heel of the print. "What's this?"

She turned the brush over, using the pointy tip of the handle to dig at something more solid than dirt in the groove. As Charlie watched, a few reddish pebbles came loose, tinkling down against the hard table.

Charlie's eyes went wide as he looked at the red pebbles, then Jeremy and Marion were leaning over his shoulders.

"Doesn't that look just like—"

"Yes, it does," Crystal said. "It looks just like the red rocks you brought back from the Franklin Park Zoo."

Crystal reached into her book bag, which was beneath the table where she was sitting, and pulled out a little plastic bag filled with the pebbles from the zoo. She opened the bag, then placed the two samples side by side on the table. Then she reached back into her bag and pulled out a colorful spiral-bound booklet—her rock-identification chart, which she'd compiled from various sources on the Internet.

Charlie had seen the chart many times before. For Crystal, it was basically the Bible, and she carried it everywhere. The booklet was divided by rock type, and then further categorized by different subsets that Charlie only vaguely understood.

"These samples are definitely similar, and probably the same. Which is quite a puzzle, because one of these came from the zoo, and the other got caught up in my plaster mold in the Public Garden. But before we get ahead of ourselves, I think we should try to identify these rocks."

She leafed her way through the first page of her booklet.

"First we need to determine if the sample is igneous, sedimentary, or metamorphic."

Charlie knew that these were the three basic categories of rock, referring mainly to where they were found and how they were formed.

Crystal lifted one of the reddish pebbles.

"Tons of texture in this sample, so it's definitely not igneous; igneous rock is formed by superhigh volcanic temperatures, which make it smooth, black, white, and gray."

Kentaro reached forward and touched one of the other reddish pebbles with his tiny hands.

"This looks more like sedimentary rock, right? Formed by deposits, mineral or organic?"

Crystal nodded. "It's not glittery or shiny, so that pretty much rules out metamorphic rock, which is also formed by high temperatures. So, yes, I'd say this is sedimentary."

"So? How does that help us?"

"It doesn't," Crystal said. "Yet. But now that we know the type of rock we've found, we have to look deeper."

"Grain size," Charlie said. "Hardness. Color. Then maybe we can identify what we've got."

Crystal nodded.

"Grain size is easy. If we'd needed a magnifying glass to see the pebble, we'd know we were dealing with something fine grained. But this is big enough for the naked eye. It's coarse."

Jeremy reached forward to grab one of the pebbles, but Crystal swatted his hand away.

"Hey, I was just going to figure out how hard it was."

"By bashing it against the table, right?" Crystal said. "I know how you think. There's no reason for theatrics."

She carefully ran her thumbnail over the reddish pebble.

"If dragging your sample across the nail produces a line on your fingernail, then you know it's not a very soft rock. A very soft rock registers a Mohs' scale—a measurement of minerals contained within the rock—of one to two. The next stage of rock can scratch fingernails, but not steel or glass. That's a Mohs' scale of three and a half to five. And when you reach the very hard stage, a Mohs' scale of six or more, we're talking rocks that can scratch glass or steel. For example, diamonds register a level 10 in hardness. And diamonds can definitely scratch glass or steel."

Kentaro took the sample from Crystal, while Marion went over to a storage closet and grabbed a glass slide from a small cardboard box. Then Kentaro carefully pushed the pebble across the slide as if he was etching an inscription. The pebble made a noise similar to the sound of a fingernail swooping across a chalkboard. Kentaro lifted the sample from the glass, revealing a perfect scratch line.

"A hard rock. Mohs' scale six or more."

"And one ruined slide," Marion added.

"Better a slide than my fingernail," Crystal said. "Let's get on with this discovery process."

She looked down at her rock book, opening to a page containing multiple subcharts filled with pictures of specific types of rocks.

"We now move on to color and composition. We've got a Mohs' of six or more, a coarse grain, sedimentary, and reddish in color. Which gives us a concretion commonly found in—"

She looked up from the book, confused.

"What is it?" Charlie asked.

"We must have done something wrong," Crystal said. "Because this doesn't make any sense."

She pointed down to a selection in her book.

Charlie read the words out loud, as his friends all read the same designation in silence.

"The African savanna."

Charlie looked at Crystal.

"The African savanna? Isn't that the vast grassland where wild animals roam? Things like lions and tigers? These pebbles are both from the African savanna? How? The boot that left this print in the Public Garden, in the middle of Boston, has been to the savanna?"

And then Charlie realized, with a start, that he'd gotten it backward. The boot hadn't somehow magically gone to the savanna—the savanna had come to Boston.

Charlie's heart began to race in his chest.

"Marion and Jeremy," he said as he rose from the bench, "you guys get to work on modeling that print. In the meantime, Crystal, Kentaro, and I are going on a little trip."

"Where to?" Crystal asked.

Charlie grinned.

"To the savanna, of course. Don't worry, you're not even going to need your passport. But you might need your subway pass."

"WHY DOES THE LITTLE guy always have to go first?"

Kentaro was halfway up the wooden fence, his neon sneakers jammed into a little crook between two of the slots, while Charlie strained beneath him, both hands pushing as hard as he could against his friend's haunches. Crystal was standing next to him, mostly for moral support; Kentaro, fully extended, had gotten both hands over the top of the pickets and was now pretty much on his own.

"Where's your adventurous spirit?" Crystal asked, her voice little more than a whisper.

It was already dark outside, and the zoo would be closing in minutes; they hadn't seen another person since they'd passed the entrance to Bird's World and made their way around the giant condor cage. But still, they knew they were taking a big risk.

"Just be glad you don't have to get malaria shots," Charlie grunted, as he gave Kentaro another push.

Gravel and sand rained down from Kentaro's shoes as he scrambled up the last few inches to the top of the fence.

"This isn't exactly legal, is it?" Kentaro whispered back down toward them, and Charlie shrugged.

"The sign says authorized personnel only. Which probably doesn't mean us. So, technically, it's trespassing. But then again, we do have zoo passes, and this is still part of the zoo. So if we get caught, we just say we didn't see the sign and we thought the fence was part of the exhibit."

"Escape from the Killer Condors," Crystal said. "Every man for himself. I'd pay extra for that."

Kentaro glared down at her.

"You still haven't told me how I'm going to get you two in after me. Even if I can find an entrance gate, what if it's locked?"

"You're industrious," Crystal said. "You'll figure something out."

Charlie had to admit, it wasn't their most detailed plan. But when he'd made the connection between the pebbles found in the boot print at the Public Garden and the under-construction exhibit at the zoo, he'd immediately known they needed to get back to Franklin Park. Somehow, this area of the zoo was related to the woolly mammoth tusk—and in some way, it all had something to do with the African savanna.

"If you can't find a gate," Charlie said, "just look around, see what you can see, then come back here. We'll figure out a way to get you back over. I saw some trees back by the kangaroos with branches we might be able to use to tow you over the top—"

Charlie was interrupted by a sudden rustling behind him. He whirled—just in time to see a large man pushing his way through the bushes that led to the condor cage. The man had a square jaw, thick dark hair, and eyes set deep above rectangular cheeks. Heck, everything about the man was cubic and right angled, down to the massive biceps bulging against the gray of his woolen sweat suit.

"What do you kids think you're doing?" the man growled, and suddenly there was more rustling behind him.

A second man came out of the brush, this one toting a flashlight. The second man was taller and skinnier than the first, and dressed entirely in green; his arms, crooked at the elbows, made him look almost like a giant praying mantis. If Charlie didn't know better, he'd have thought the man was part insect.

"I think you'd better come down from there," the second man said, catching Kentaro in the conic beam from the flashlight. "Before someone gets hurt."

Charlie wasn't sure if the man had meant the words to be menacing. But as Kentaro slowly worked his way back down to the dirt next to him, he could feel his throat seizing up, a lump working its way down his esophagus.

Charlie had been in dangerous situations before, but usually he at least understood what he was up against. This time he had no idea who these men were—but they weren't wearing anything zoo related. If they were security guards, they were the strangest-looking guards he'd ever seen.

"Sorry," Crystal said, thinking on her feet. "We were playing around by the birds, and I tossed my favorite rock over this fence. My friend was just trying to help recover it; it's really nice, a crystal, like my name. Crystal."

"Didn't you see the sign?" the man in green asked.

Crystal glanced down the fence.

"Sign? Wow, whoops, must have missed that. Honest misunderstanding. We'll be on our way."

The square man looked them over, then glanced at his insectoid friend.

"I don't think so," he said ominously.

• • •

Ten minutes later Charlie, Crystal, and Kentaro found themselves standing in the middle of a partially constructed domelike building, looking out through flaps of tarp at the surrounding reddish dunes, which rose and fell all the way to the fence they had just attempted to climb. The walk over from the padlocked gate—twenty feet down from where they had tried to make their surreptitious approach—had gone by in terrifying silence. Although the two men hadn't touched them, prodding them along with the cone of light from the flashlight and a lot of violent pointing—there was no mistaking their malevolent mood. It seemed that these two men wanted nothing more than for one of the three kids to make a break for it, and no doubt they'd have easily chased them down. Then—who knows? Charlie had no idea why they'd been taken inside the construction site, or what the men wanted.

The under-construction building, if you could call it that, was still mostly insulation, two-by-fours, and foam padding, lit by a handful of bare lightbulbs hanging from the arched ceiling. Without the lightbulbs, they'd have had to rely on the flashlight; the sky had gone from gray to dark, and though at that time of the year that could mean anywhere from five to seven p.m., they were clearly well past the zoo's closing hours.

"Our parents are going to be looking for us," Charlie said, his voice quivering. He was shaking all over, and he was pretty sure it had nothing to do with the cold.

The insectoid man was about to answer when another voice broke through the darkness.

"No reason to be concerned," a man's voice said, with the hint of an English accent. "This will only take a few minutes, and then we can all be on our way. I'm just curious why the three of you seemed so intent on climbing my fence."

The voice was followed by the man, who stepped beneath one of the tarp's flaps and into the domelike building. The man was well dressed in a gray flannel suit and matching tie, and even in the dim light from the naked bulbs, Charlie could see that his face was tanned and lined, almost like leather. Above his sky-blue eyes, he had a shock of almost-white blond hair.

He crossed the room in front of them and paused by a mahogany table that was pressed up against one of the still-under-construction walls. At first Charlie had been too terrified to notice, but on the table sat a large spherical globe on a metal base. Charlie briefly caught sight of other objects on the table: something long, slightly curved, and white, next to a coffee cup emblazoned with a word he could barely make out, something that started with

"LON." But then the man placed a palm on the globe, gave it a good spin, and Charlie's attention was diverted. The sphere spun and spun and spun, a mesmerizing blur.

"I know my associates can be a little blunt," the man continued, signaling the two other men to leave the room.

The square, bulky man exited first, barely giving Charlie and his friends a glance. But the insectlike thug paused by the tarp, glaring at Charlie for a full beat, before exiting as well.

"But sometimes a blunt instrument is as valuable as a sword," he said.

Then he grinned.

"I'm sorry, I haven't introduced myself. My name is Blake Headstrom. And this place, where you attempted to trespass, is my newest project."

"Mr. Headstrom," Crystal tried. "We didn't mean to trespass. We were only—"

"Curious?" Headstrom interrupted. "I completely understand. And I don't mean to frighten you, you're not in trouble. Really, it's just the accent. My family is from London, though I grew up just about everywhere else. But that's neither here nor there."

He stepped away from the spinning globe, beckoning Charlie and his friends to follow. Then he reached for the tarp, holding it up for them so they could exit the dome first.

"Since you seem so eager to see the exhibit before it's open to the general public, I should give you a guided tour."

Charlie felt the shaking in his body beginning to subside. Apparently, they weren't in trouble.

Although this man seemed odd—and the fact that he had henchmen seemed even odder—he didn't appear to be angry with them for trying to climb the fence. In fact, he seemed almost pleasant.

Charlie went through the tarp first, followed by Kentaro. Crystal lingered behind, moving close to the table with the globe, then followed.

Once outside, there was no sign of the square or insectlike thugs, just sweeping, reddish dunes. Headstrom waited until they were all next to him, then started forward, taking them around to the other side of the domed building.

"You've already seen the sandy Sahara; this other side is going to be more savanna—grassy, low reeds, even a man-made oasis over by those palm trees."

He pointed ahead, but Charlie could hardly see anything in the darkness. If Headstrom was having similar visual issues, he didn't show it; he just kept moving, his feet following a gravel path between low patches of plant life that had already started to grow amidst the reddish dirt.

"Over there"—Headstrom pointed to a far patch of dense-looking tree life—"we're going to put in a jungle. But not just any jungle."

Past the trees, Charlie could make out a huge pile of wooden crates.

"It's going to be perfectly authentic, with items straight from Africa."

"Those crates are from Africa?" Crystal asked. Charlie knew she was thinking about the pebbles they had pulled from the boot print. No doubt they had come from this place—and they had been found right by the woolly mammoth tusk.

"Yes, indeed. And they contain the most magnificent, authentic samples of African savanna, jungle, and desert geology and fauna. You see, I'm a world traveler, but I know most people don't have the freedom to live like I have. So my goal is to bring the world to them. Starting with Africa."

Charlie looked at the man's leathery face. He was practically beaming, and though there was still something odd about the way he spoke, his words seemed genuine. Charlie couldn't fault his goals.

"That sounds amazing," Charlie said.

"Amazing, and authentic," Headstrom said. "It's always been my dream to re-create this environment as exactly as I can. The beauty of Africa is beyond exquisite. And I think when we open, people are going to enjoy the experience."

The two henchmen had appeared again, both with flashlights this time, and were lighting the way back toward the gate that led to the rest of the zoo.

"But now it's getting late, and I think your parents will be worried. My associates, Gareth and Grill, will happily show you back to the parking lot."

And with that, he turned and headed back toward the under-construction dome. Charlie watched him go, until the insectlike thug—Grill—waved his flashlight, beckoning them forward.

It was another twenty minutes of silent hiking before the two henchmen got them to the main exit to the zoo, a pair of turnstiles that led out into the parking area. Charlie could see his mother's minivan already waiting for them, his mother sitting behind the wheel, happily leafing through a copy of *Scientific American*. If she had even noticed that they were coming out of the zoo well past closing time, she didn't seem concerned. A benefit—and detriment—of having an absentminded professor for a parent.

As Charlie led his friends toward the car, Crystal grabbed his arm, slowing his progress. When he looked toward her, she reached into her front pocket and pulled something out—something long and white and curved.

Charlie's eyes went wide.

"You grabbed that off the desk?" Charlie gasped. Kentaro turned at the words, staring at Crystal as well.

"I didn't think anyone would notice, and I was right," Crystal said.

She held the object in front of her, so that both of them could see. Charlie knew instantly what it was.

"A piece of tusk," he said quietly. There was no way to know if it was also woolly mammoth, but it was way too much of a coincidence—them finding a mammoth tusk in the Public Garden, alongside a boot print with African savanna dirt in its grooves. And a tusk sitting in the middle of Headstrom's under-construction savanna exhibit.

Curiouser, and curiouser, and curiouser.

Crystal grinned, then slid the piece of tusk back into her pocket.

"Indeed," she said, mimicking an English accent.

"SO THEY CAME OUT of nowhere? Dragged you down from the fence? I'm surprised you didn't wet your pants!"

Jeremy was speaking in a stage whisper over the circular computer table in the back corner of the Nagassack Middle School library. This coveted corner had always been where the Whiz Kids gathered between third-period English and fourth-period math, trying not to catch the attention of the school librarian, Mr. Scarborough. The bane of their existence, he was a rule-obsessed, finicky, bespectacled man who would have happily given them all detention if he'd caught Jeremy speaking too loudly or, worse yet, the five of them using one of the school's computers for something that was decidedly not school oriented. But, thankfully, Scarborough was nowhere to be seen. The man was probably lodged in his back office, researching more rules he could apply to what was already the school's most legislated quiet zone.

But if you needed computer access during school hours, there was no place else to go; and at the moment Charlie and his friends knew that the next step in their investigation involved a whole lot of Google.

At the moment, the library was mostly empty. Charlie spotted a few kids sitting in the "gazebo," the rounded, sunken central structure at the heart of the library, about a dozen feet in diameter, containing a few beanbag chairs and a little stage for readings; but other than that, they had the place to themselves. The utilitarian turquoise carpeting that covered nearly every surface of the library, a throwback that probably hadn't been updated since the disco era, muffled most of the sound—but even so, it wouldn't do them any good to speak in anything more than a throaty whisper.

"They didn't drag me down," Kentaro said, whispering next to Charlie. "They asked me to come down. But they were pretty scary."

"Why does a developer need security guards?" Marion asked.

He was plugging away at the computer, which they'd signed out from the row of laptops by the checkout desk, because he was the most skilled of the group at data retrieval. Sometimes it was hard to tell if his eyes were red because he'd spent the entire night browsing art and architecture sites online or because of the pollen count in the air.

"I don't think they were security guards. Headstrom kept calling them his 'associates,' but I think they were more like paid thugs. Or maybe mercenaries."

"You're not far off," Marion said, suddenly turning the computer so they could all see what he'd found. He'd spent nearly forty minutes on the computer before they'd arrived—ditching most of English class under the guise of an allergic reaction to some bad mushrooms in his breakfast omelet—and had gone back and forth between his continuing work on scanning the plaster boot print, and the new task of researching Headstrom. Though the boot print was taking more time than he'd expected, his work on Headstrom had already borne fruit.

In the center of the screen was a picture of Headstrom. Though the photo was from a time when the man was much younger, Charlie had no trouble recognizing the ice-blond hair or the leathery face. In the photo, Headstrom was standing above the carcass of a dead lion, his hand resting on the butt of a long hunting rifle. The caption above the photo was no less frightening than the picture:

For multimillionaire adventurer Blake Headstrom, big-game hunting isn't just a hobby; it's also a way of life.

"He hunts lions?" Crystal gasped. "He told us that he's a fan of the African savanna."

"Oh, yes," Marion said, reading through the article. "He's quite a fan. According to this, twenty years ago he made an enormous fortune leading wealthy hunters on savanna tours. Although he was born in London, like he told you, he grew up mostly in Africa, and he used the skills and connections he'd accrued to put together hunting expeditions to the farthest reaches of the continent, chasing down lions, zebras, even elephants."

"Elephants?" Charlie said. "I thought elephants were endangered. And that killing elephants for sport was illegal."

"It is now," Marion said. "It didn't used to be. And according to this next article . . ."

Marion used the keyboard to flip to another page.

"Sometime over the past five years, Headstrom segued into a new line of work. Now he builds exhibits at zoos. Elaborate exhibits, from the looks of some of his work. In London, he actually put up an entire waterfall that's supposed to look a bit like the Victoria Falls—the highest waterfall on the entire African continent. It cost him a fortune."

"He must have made a lot of money on those hunting trips," Kentaro said, clearly disgusted. But Marion shook his head.

"Nowhere near enough to fund all this. Look what I found."

Marion glanced over his shoulder, making sure nobody had approached while he was talking.

Then he flicked more keys and opened up an entirely new file.

"Remember the triangulation I was doing on our first visit to the zoo?"

"Not this again," Jeremy said.

"Yes, this again. Well, I was able to use the measurements I made to cross-reference a search of construction permits across the country. And I found something interesting."

He turned the computer around again, showing the group. Displayed on the monitor was a map of the

United States. The map was yellow, with a black border to delineate each state. Across the map, Charlie could see a dozen red markings, each in a different state.

"Each of these markings is another construction project of Headstrom Industries. We're talking twelve different massive exhibits, in twelve different cities. All of them in zoos, all of them African-savanna related."

"What does this mean?" Crystal asked.

"I don't know," Marion answered, "but this sort of construction must cost a fortune. Nothing I've found can explain how he's funding all of this. He's rich—but not that rich."

Crystal reached below the table and retrieved the white fragment of tusk she'd taken from Headstrom's project at the Franklin Park Zoo.

"Well, it might have something to do with this. You think he's selling mammoth ivory to pay for all these exhibits?"

Marion shook his head.

"I thought of that too, but there's no way. Even though mammoth ivory is worth a ton of money, selling it in bulk is almost impossible. There just isn't enough mammoth ivory available to raise this kind of cash. And if Headstrom was in possession of so many woolly mammoth tusks, someone would have written about it.

It all comes from the Arctic, and every big haul makes news."

Crystal held the piece of tusk in front of the computer screen. In the light coming from the pixels, it appeared even more white than the sample they had found in the Public Garden. Charlie couldn't be sure, but he thought the new sample looked a little different.

"I think we should bring this to Dr. Church and carbon-date it as well. Maybe we can figure out if it's from the same place as the other piece. Maybe he really did find some large haul of mammoth ivory, and he's selling it to fund his projects."

"Or maybe something else is going on," Crystal said. There was a dark look in her eyes.

"Headstrom spent a large part of his life killing animals, and now he's become a lover of the African savanna? Something about this doesn't sit well with me. Something's off about that man—and it's not just his accent."

Charlie didn't respond, but deep down, he had a feeling that Crystal was right.

TO CHARLIE NUMBERS, THERE was nothing more magical than the science of pulleys and levers. Many times he'd spent a Saturday morning at the Science in the Park Exhibit at the Museum of Science, trying to lift a two-ton block of steel attached to a series of ropes at different leverage points—finally achieving the feat, in what felt like a miracle. But Charlie had always known there was nothing miraculous about it; though, often, science and math did indeed feel like magic, and magic, after all, was the basis of miracles.

Standing outside in a corner of the grassy Quad on the Tufts University campus in Medford, just twenty minutes outside of Boston, Charlie was lost in thought of miracles and magic as he looked up at the massive bronze statue of Jumbo the Elephant: both a mascot to the university, whose students called themselves "Jumbos," and a part of the place's history, because not only was it a marvel of metal sculpture work, but it was also based on a real live animal, whose hide had once been one of the campus's prized collectibles.

The story of Jumbo was poignant to Charlie, especially considering the events of the past two weeks that had led him to this place.

In the late 1800s, Jumbo was more than just an elephant: The centerpiece of the greatest circus on Earth, P. T. Barnum's traveling show, Jumbo was heralded as the largest elephant in the world, and certainly the most famous. Unfortunately, on September 15, 1885, Jumbo met with tragedy when he was run over by a freight train. Although his skeleton ended up in the American Museum of Natural History in New York, the elephant itself was restored by a taxidermist and was brought to Tufts to act as a mascot for all the school's sports teams. That might have been the end of the story—except for another bout of tragedy. In 1975, the stuffed elephant was caught in a mysterious fire and was burned to ash. Luckily, an intrepid administrative assistant scraped up some of the ashes and placed them in a Peter Pan Crunchy Peanut Butter jar, which was hidden away in a safe in the athletic department, where it remained to this day.

Although the elephant himself had been reduced to ashes, Tufts had never forgotten Jumbo. The statue in front of where Charlie now stood—all five thousand pounds of it—was a daily reminder of the magnificent animal and what he meant to the community.

Charlie wasn't just amazed at the beauty of the statue; he was also awed by the technology that had allowed such a massive homage to be transported to the Quad. It took a combination of engineering and art, employing pulleys and leverage, to move something that by its nature might have seemed impossible to move.

"It's quite amazing," Mrs. Hennigan said as she came up behind Charlie. He was on his own tonight, his friends unable to come up with enough excuses to get them out on yet another school night. Charlie felt a mixed feeing of luck and sadness that his parents might not have even noticed he was gone, as they were so caught up in their own work. He was glad, at least, to have his oddball teacher with him.

"There's just something about elephants," she continued. "They say that once you've met one in person, you're never the same. Did you know that mother elephants who lose children actually mourn their young?"

"Really?" Charlie asked. He didn't know that much

about elephants, other than what he'd learned in school: that they traveled in groups, that they cared for their young, that they were very smart and endangered.

"Yes, mother elephants will return to the spot where a child has died, again and again, year after year. They're wonderful creatures, almost as smart as people. It's such a shame that they've been hunted almost out of existence."

Charlie nodded, pulling awkwardly at his sleeves. He was wearing his favorite blue-and-white-striped shirt underneath a navy down coat, which was uncomfortable, but seemed to fit in perfectly with all the college students milling about. Blue and brown seemed to be popular choices for clothing colors. Of course, Mrs. Hennigan was once again in beige, from head to toe.

"It's fitting that Dr. Church is speaking here tonight," Mrs. Hennigan continued, leading Charlie around the statue of Jumbo toward the entrance to one of the buildings on the corner of the Quad. "Cabot Center is the lecture setting of choice for visiting professors, but a statue of an elephant is the best press Dr. Church could ask for."

As Charlie followed Mrs. Hennigan into the auditorium, he guessed that Church wasn't in need of any press: the three-hundred-seat theater was packed, the bright halogen ceiling lights illuminating more than fifteen completely full rows of seats.

Dr. Church was at the head of the lecture hall, standing in front of a whiteboard and a projection screen. As Charlie and Mrs. Hennigan entered, an artist's rendition of a re-created woolly mammoth was on the screen. Charlie felt a thrill move through him as they found seats at the back of the room.

Dr. Church began his lecture. The talk wasn't geared toward kids, but Charlie was rapt with attention through the entire thing. Charlie didn't understand everything that the scientist said, but he got the gist of the talk, which was basically about the similarities between elephants and mammoths, and how those similarities would one day make it possible for Dr. Church and his team to bring back the prehistoric beasts.

As it turned out, mammoths and elephants weren't very different at all. In fact, they were so closely related that if a mammoth were to somehow come back to life, it would be able to have children with a modern elephant. The main difference was that mammoths liked the cold. They were happiest when they were trampling down frozen tundra, which in turn was actually good for the environment; the process kept the tundra cool, and could help the world from getting too hot. Bringing back the woolly mammoth wasn't just something fun to think about; if Dr. Church could succeed in bringing back a herd of mammoths, he could actually help solve the climate crisis.

It was heady stuff, and Charlie knew he was getting only a touch of what Dr. Church was saying, but when Dr. Church finished the lecture by referencing the statue outside, and how just recently the Ringling Bros. Circus had donated its elephants (which were no longer performing, for ethical reasons) to Dr. Church's project, Charlie roared along with the rest of the crowd.

Watching Dr. Church come off the stage was like watching a rock star end a show, and to Charlie it was awesome. He loved science, but he'd never thought a scientist could be a rock star.

After most of the audience left, Charlie followed Mrs. Hennigan toward the stage. Dr. Church was still surrounded by well-wishers, so for the moment Charlie would have to wait. He could feel the piece of tusk that Crystal had taken from Headstrom's construction site pressing against the pocket of his slacks; he was dying to show the object to Dr. Church, to see if he could match it to the sample they'd gotten from the Public Garden, but he knew he had to be patient.

As they got closer to Dr. Church, the aisle leading

down to the stage became more crowded; Charlie felt himself jostled on both sides by students, and for a moment he found himself separated from Mrs. Hennigan. He hurried forward, trying to catch sight of her beige on beige, when instead he saw someone heading right toward him.

It took him a moment to recognize the young Asian woman he had seen in Dr. Church's lab the last time he'd visited. She was wearing a long overcoat and a baseball hat pulled low over her eyes, but it was definitely the same woman. And she seemed to zero in on Charlie, which immediately made him nervous. She still looked too young to be a student of Dr. Church's, but if she was someone's daughter, what was she doing at the lecture by herself?

Charlie searched for Mrs. Hennigan, but she was far ahead now, almost to the stage. Charlie looked to his left and saw an emergency exit at the end of a row of empty seats. He made a quick decision and started down the row.

He'd made it halfway when he lost his fight against the urge to look back. The young woman was right behind him, closing in fast.

Charlie hit the emergency exit with his shoulder, and the door flung open, depositing him back into the Quad, just a few feet from the bronze Jumbo. He took two steps toward the statue, when a hand touched his shoulder.

"Hold on. I just want to ask you a couple of questions."

Charlie stopped, turning to face the young woman. Up close, she looked even younger; she couldn't have been older than sixteen. She had a wide face and almond eyes, and her lips looked drawn in with a red crayon.

"Who are you? And why are you following me?"

"Alice Yang, and, actually, I'm not. I mean, I wasn't, until I saw you at the lecture. I'm shadowing Dr. Church for a project I'm working on. I'm a junior reporter at Channel 7 News."

Charlie raised his eyebrows. A television network was hiring high school kids as reporters? But he decided not to press her on the subject; after all, he was just a sixth grader and he'd done some pretty amazing things in his life already. Maybe Yang was some sort of media prodigy. Or maybe her mother owned the television studio. Charlie wasn't the type to judge a person on her age.

"You're doing a story on Dr. Church?"

A group of college students exiting the lecture walked by, and the young woman paused to let them pass. After they were gone, she pulled Charlie around the edge of the bronze statue so that they were hidden by Jumbo's oversize curved trunk.

"Not exactly," she said, conspiratorially.

"Then why are you here?"

She pointed up at the bronze elephant.

"I'm here for him, actually."

She reached behind herself and swung a saddlebag around from where it had been hanging against the low of her back. Charlie saw a circular logo emblazoned on one side. It was peeling a little at the edge, but he still recognized it as the symbol of one of his parents' favorite television news shows—the Channel 7 Spotlight—which he'd watched along with them a few times. It highlighted investigative stories, local and national, but usually with a Boston connection. He'd never seen Alice Yang on the show before, but seeing the logo on her bag put him a little bit more at ease. Maybe she really was who she said she was.

Alice reached into her bag and pulled out a yellow notepad. On the cover she'd pasted a handful of photos of elephants; unfortunately, the elephants were all lying on their sides, missing their tusks.

"I'm chasing a story about elephant ivory. You know that elephants are endangered, right? And that it's illegal to kill them for their ivory? But it still happens. And that ivory is making its way into our country—into our city—and is being sold to be used in jewelry, shady medicines, all sorts of things. I've been tracking an upsurge in ivory that's found its way into Boston and about a dozen other cities across the country."

She opened her notepad to a hand-drawn map of the United States. In various places on the map, she'd drawn large Xs.

"Chicago, Austin, Houston, Miami, Kansas City, San Francisco—this is going on all over the country. An influx of illegal elephant ivory being sold for large amounts of money."

Charlie stared at the map, at the pattern of Xs. He knew that human brains were designed to recognize patterns; it was an evolutionary advantage, because the better an animal was at recognizing patterns, the more likely that animal was to be able to predict, and avoid, danger. Because of this, people often searched for patterns where there weren't any.

But Charlie was sure he'd seen this particular pattern before.

"So someone is selling illegal tusks in all these cities?"

Alice nodded.

"When I saw the sample you'd brought to the Church Lab, I thought it might have something to do with my investigation. But then when Dr. Church identified it as woolly mammoth, I realized it was something else. Mammoth ivory isn't illegal and doesn't lead to dead elephants."

Charlie retrieved the piece of tusk from his pocket, turning it over in his hands. He was still thinking about that familiar pattern of Xs.

"I brought this piece for Dr. Church to analyze as well. I think it's also mammoth."

"Why? Did you find it in the same place as the other one?"

"Not exactly. But it's somehow related. The thing is—even if it is mammoth ivory, I think it's also related to your investigation."

Alice's face tightened, and she reached out and touched Charlie's arm.

"Why?"

Charlie took a breath, then glanced up at Jumbo. Such a noble creature, so beautiful and powerful and even soulful. The idea that people could kill these creatures just to take their tusks was hard to accept. No matter how much money that ivory might be worth, sharing the world with creatures like Jumbo would always be worth much, much more.

He turned back to the junior reporter.

"I need to show you something," he said. "And I think it's going to crack your investigation wide open."

"I CAN'T BELIEVE WE'RE doing this," Janice said in a low voice as she moved her chair up close to where Charlie was sitting, between Alice Yang and Rod. They were on a circular, leather recessed sofa in the back corner of one of the poshest lobbies Charlie had ever set foot in. "I mean, digging around the Public Garden is one thing, but confronting a potential ivory smuggler right in his office, in the center of the Financial District . . . I feel like James Bond."

"That would be Janice Bond," Rod said, and snickered, but even he seemed to be cowed by the overbearing setting, his normally wide shoulders curved in toward his chest as if he was trying to make himself look smaller in the vast, open waiting area. "And I think it has a nice ring to it. Alice, no offense, I know you're on television and everything, but do you really think this is a good idea? Ambushing the man right in his office? I mean, according to Charlie and his nerd patrol, this guy shoots lions for fun. You think he's going to take this sitting down from a bunch of kids? Again, no offense."

Charlie shifted nervously against the leather couch. He looked around the lobby; everything was done in chrome, from the huge security desk in the center of the vast room, staffed by a half dozen men in uniform, to the arched ceilings, at least twenty feet above. The three glass revolving doors that led out into the narrow streets of Boston's Financial District glinted in the morning light, as they fed a constant stream of men and women in business suits toward the bank of elevators along the back wall.

He shifted his gaze to Alice Yang. She still had her saddlebag against her side, with the Channel 7 logo, and on her lap sat a small video camera. Not the sort of thing Charlie would have expected from a TV reporter; more like something he might have found in the AV room at Nagassack Middle. The device could fit in the palm of his hand and was attached to a telescoping tripod that was now folded into the camera's base.

Alice looked almost as nervous as Charlie felt. She

had traded her baseball cap for a tight ponytail, and though she was wearing a dress, she was also wearing boots that had little Hello Kitty emblems imprinted right above the heel. Charlie had never seen a television reporter wearing Hello Kitty before, but then again, he didn't watch that much TV.

"It's what we call in the business the direct approach," Alice said. "We hit him with the truth, right on camera, and he can't possibly deny it."

Although she seemed nervous, she also seemed determined. In fact, she had the same look in her eyes that Charlie had first seen when he'd brought Alice to the Nagassack library the morning after Church's lecture, and Marion had shown her the map on his computer, of all the savanna exhibits that Headstrom Industries was constructing across the country. Even a fool could see that the exhibits matched up exactly to the Xs on Alice's map; Blake Headstrom was building African savanna parks in the same dozen cities that were seeing an influx of illegal elephant ivory.

Charlie didn't think it was enough to make any conclusions, but Alice had immediately jumped on the connection. She'd gone to work tracking down Headstrom's business offices—located right in the middle of Boston, in a grandiose glass and steel tower amidst the porcupine spikes of the financial center—and had made an appointment to see the man, face-to-face. She'd made up some story about doing a show about adventure travel, focusing on the savanna; but her intention, to Charlie, was obvious. She was determined to break her story with an on-camera confession.

Charlie had met Headstrom; the man was slick. Charlie doubted he would confess anything, even if he was involved. But he couldn't pass up the chance to see the interaction in person. He hadn't intended to invite Janice along. In fact, he'd kept the rest of his friends out of the meeting because he wasn't sure how Headstrom was going to react, and accusing a businessman of a crime could get dicey. He didn't want to put any of his friends in danger, or get them in trouble. But he'd actually reached out to Janice about something else—another step in their investigation—and when he'd told her about Alice and the upcoming visit to Headstrom's offices, she'd demanded to come along. "Sounds too exciting to miss," she'd said.

"And besides, you'll see, sometimes my chair can make people more honest than they mean to be. They feel sorry, then they overcompensate. It's like a magic wand."

Charlie wasn't sure exactly what she meant, but deep down he was happy she was with him. And for once he wasn't upset that Rod was there as well. Not only because Rod was twice his size and more likely to stand a chance if Headstrom's henchmen showed up, but because whether he knew it or not, Rod was actually instrumental to the next leg of Charlie's quest.

But the next part of his mission would have to wait, because at that moment one of the uniformed security guards gestured to them from the desk, then pointed to the bank of elevators.

"Elevator 4. Mr. Headstrom's assistant will meet you on the twenty-second floor."

Alice grabbed her video camera and her saddlebag, then leaped off the couch.

"Here we go," she said with a smile. But Charlie could see the slight tinge of fear in her eyes.

The twenty-second-floor lobby was almost as luxe as the first: sky-high ceilings lacquered in chrome, vast picture windows offering a panoramic view of the entire Boston skyline, all the way to the harbor on one side and the Charles River on the other. There was another security desk, this one shiny and black, maybe even obsidian, staffed by two women in matching light blue uniforms with badges that said Headstrom Industries in twisty gold letters. But Charlie and his group weren't there for very long; within ten seconds of the elevator doors opening, they were met by a tall, skinny woman with short dark hair, snugly wrapped in a crisp white Armani pantsuit.

"Mr. Headstrom is always excited to talk to the local press," she said, as she led them down a carpeted hallway toward a pair of mahogany doors. "When we're finally ready to open our exhibits, we're planning a nationwide media tour. Bringing the African savanna to America has always been his dream, and we know television reporters like you are going to be part of what allows him to achieve that dream."

The woman paused as she reached the doors, glancing down at Alice's boots.

"Though we were a bit surprised to get a call from your direct line, Ms. Yang. We usually set these things up directly through the network's publicity department."

Alice brushed past the woman as the doors swung inward on their own.

"Yes, usually that's the way it works, but I'm on deadline," she said, and before the woman could respond she was through the doorway.

Charlie hurried behind her, Janice and Rod right after him.

Headstrom's office was immense, an entire corner

of the skyscraper, with windows that ran from the floor all the way to the ceiling. Charlie could see all the way to the airport; at the moment a jet was lifting off the runway, glistening in the light flashing up from the waters of the harbor. Closer, he could see the cargo ships lined up by the wharfs that lined the older part of the seaport, and even closer, the pretty new buildings that were going up along the waterfront, the hotels, restaurants, bars, and even shopping malls that were transforming an entire section of the city, day by day.

Closer, closer, there was a two-seater couch up against the window, and then directly across, Headstrom's desk, a massive wooden trunk of wood that looked as if it had been carted right to Boston from the African jungle. It was flat and rectangular on top, but the base was curved, still covered in bark, resting on four ornate wooden legs. On top of the desk sat two computers, a Xerox machine, a trio of phones, and a huge glass cylinder. Within the cylinder stood something Charlie immediately recognized: a single tusk, about the length of his right arm. Unlike the object he'd dropped off with Dr. Church at the lecture at Tufts, or the object he and his friends had found in the Public Garden, the tusk in the cylinder was not a fragment but a much larger specimen. At around three feet long, it couldn't have been from an adult mammoth—or elephant, for that matter—but from a smaller female, or a child. Even so, it was incredible, and Charlie was so entranced by the tusk that he didn't notice the mahogany doors clicking shut behind them.

"Well, this is certainly a surprise."

Charlie turned and saw Headstrom step forward from a recessed corner of his office. He was holding a large photo book, something involving African hanging masks. He was wearing a herringbone suit, with a white scarf instead of a tie, and his equally white hair was swept back from his lined, tan forehead.

"Ms. Yang, I presume. I'm Blake Headstrom. I've already met at least one of your companions."

Headstrom closed the book with a bang, staring right at Charlie. The man seemed to be trying to decide what Charlie's presence in his office might mean. But then he shrugged it off, maybe because his attention had turned to Janice, who had wheeled over to get a better look at the cylinder on his desk.

"Unfortunately," Alice suddenly interrupted, holding her camera up in front of her, the lens trained on Headstrom's face, "this isn't a social call. I'm investigating a story about the illegal ivory trade. And we've come into possession of evidence that connects your savanna projects with a surge in ivory sales in certain cities all across the country."

Headstrom looked at the camera—and then smiled.

"That's because there is a connection," he said. "But it's not what you think."

And then he moved toward his desk. Alice kept the camera trained on him, but Charlie could see that her hands were shaking.

"When I researched cities for the placement of my savanna projects, one of the parameters I looked into was public interest in African-based jewelry. You see, my thinking was, the bigger the local market for African art, masks, and, yes, ivory jewelry, the more there would be local interest in a savanna exhibit. So you are correct; my construction projects probably do align with an upsurge in ivory."

Charlie watched as Alice slowly lowered the camera. Her entire face seemed to sag; her "ambush" hadn't gone at all as she'd expected. Headstrom hadn't confessed—quite the opposite. He'd offered a perfectly good explanation as to why his construction projects lined up with Alice's map of ivory sales.

Charlie felt his own cheeks growing red; he'd led the reporter to Headstrom, and apparently, he'd been wrong about the man. Still, it didn't explain the connection between Headstrom's savanna and the woolly mammoth tusk.

"But what about this?" Janice said, still looking up at the glass cylinder. "Isn't this illegal ivory?"

Headstrom laughed.

"My, you're a suspicious lot."

He crossed to the desk, skirting around Janice's wheelchair, and then carefully raised the glass to reveal the three-foot tusk in all its glory. Then he took the tusk in both hands and gingerly lifted it off its base.

"Let me show you something. You, sir, you seem like a strong lad."

Headstrom held the tusk out toward Rod, who glanced at Janice.

"Go ahead," Janice said.

Rod shrugged, then took the tusk from Headstrom. Headstrom quickly crossed to the printer on his desk, flicked it on, then gestured for Rod to bring the tusk nearer.

"Place the flat end on the copy glass," he said, watching as Rod complied.

White light flashed from the machine as a green glass bar moved across the glass, scanning the base of the tusk. Seconds later a black-and-white photocopy was spit out the side of the printer.

Headstrom took the paper and held it up to the light streaming in from the windows, so all the room could see. The circular base of the tusk was clearly visible; across the middle of the circle, there was a crosshatched pattern of lines, which came together in a sort of triangle, forming what looked like a perfectly sketched teepee.

"This pattern is made up of what veterinary scientists call Schreger lines. In elephant ivory, the Schreger lines meet at a more than one-hundred-degree angle. Can any of you tell me what the angle is in the lines on this printout?"

Charlie didn't need a protractor to do the calculations.

"Clearly less than ninety degrees," he said.

"Correct." Headstrom grinned. "Not just a curious boy, but also a smart one. Schreger lines of less than a hundred degrees signify a very different form of ivory, from a very different sort of tusk. This, my friends, isn't illegal elephant ivory—it's woolly mammoth."

Charlie felt a warmth move through his chest.

"You keep mammoth ivory on your desk?"

Headstrom took the tusk back from Rod and carefully placed it back into the glass cylinder.

"I'm a collector. As you may know, mammoth tusks are perfectly legal, because mammoths aren't endangered, they're extinct. And, in fact, there are close to a hundred and fifty million woolly mammoths buried in the Arctic Circle, more of them being unearthed every day. It's a beautiful, and legal, alternative to elephant ivory. And the more of it that gets harvested, the more elephants we save."

He reached forward and hit a button on the side of his desk. The mahogany doors swung open—and Charlie turned to see Gareth and Grill, Headstrom's two "associates," standing in the open doorway. Gareth was square as ever, jammed into a light blue suit that seemed two sizes too small. And Grill was still wearing green, this time a polo shirt open at the neck and golfer's slacks.

"Like you," Headstrom said toward Alice, still grinning, "my friends and I are animal lovers. We're just trying to do our part to ensure the safety of our endangered friends. That's the whole purpose of my savannas: to give everyone the opportunity to see the beauty of this natural environment before it's too late. In that light, I wish you all the best with your investigation, and if there's any way I can help, don't hesitate to visit me again."

Then, as Gareth and Grill held the doors open, clearly signaling that it was time for them all to leave, Headstrom leaned toward Charlie.

"At least this time you came through the front door, instead of trying to climb my fence. We'll call that an improvement."

With that, the man turned on his heel. As Janice rolled by him, he gave her a condescending pat on the head. For a brief moment Charlie thought Rod was going to sock the man—but, instead, Rod sullenly followed Janice through the doors.

Back in the main lobby of the building, as soon as Gareth and Grill had deposited them by the circular couches and returned to the elevators, Alice slammed the camera down and shook her head, her ponytail slapping back and forth.

"I'm so stupid," she said. "I always do this. I get so excited about something that I don't think it through."

Charlie stared, seeing tears welling in the young woman's eyes. Janice was staring at the reporter as well. Only Rod was looking away, too embarrassed by the emotional display to even make a snarky remark.

"This must happen all the time," Charlie tried, feeling bad, because this was really his fault. "Reporters chase leads that go nowhere—"

"I'm not a reporter," Alice said, dropping to the couch next to her camera.

"What about that bag? It's so official-looking," Charlie said, pointing to her messenger bag.

"This thing?" she said, wiping a tear from her cheek as she reached down and ripped the logo patch off the front, holding it up in the air.

Rod was now unable to keep his glance away.

"It's all fake. I'm not really a reporter. I took this thing off one of my sister's old bags. She's the one who works for Channel 7. I've been in her shadow my whole life, and I thought this was finally my chance to break something big, to get on air."

Janice leaned forward in her chair.

"Your sister—is your sister Cheryl Yang?"

"Who's Cheryl Yang?" Rod asked.

"Only one of the top morning anchors in the city," Janice said. "My parents watch her every day."

"Sorry, I only get the Cartoon Network," Rod said. "So your sister is a big-shot TV talking head, and you figured you could get on air chasing down some bogus story on illegal ivory?"

"It's not bogus. My research is sound. I found most of it on my sister's computer. One of her producers was following the trail of the ivory story before he decided to give up. From there I pieced together the rest by cold calling jewelry stores that traffic in elephant ivory.

And I really thought Headstrom was involved."

Charlie watched the tears running down the young woman's cheeks, then shook his head.

"Maybe he is," Charlie said. "We still don't know for sure that the tusk we found at his construction site is the same as the tusk in his office. And his story seems possible—that he's putting savanna parks in places where people are buying African jewelry, including ivory, because that's where the interest is—but it could also be a cover. There's still the mystery of how he's funding all his construction; nobody has any idea where all his money is coming from. Illegal ivory would fill that gap nicely."

"But we don't have any evidence," Janice said. "We just have a series of coincidences."

Charlie nodded.

"That's actually why I called you in the first place," he said.

"You think I can help you find evidence?" she said, surprised. "My wheelchair might be a magic wand, but I can't wave it and make evidence appear."

That got even Alice to smile, as she wiped away her tears. Charlie shook his head.

"I wasn't calling you for your chair, or for your help. I was calling you to get to your next-door neighbor."

Rod looked up.

"Me?"

"Unfortunately." Charlie grinned. "Yes. I think you might hold the key to the next step in our investigation. And although it's not the Channel 7 morning news, it does involve a camera."

THE ROOM WAS LITTLE more than a cell, dark and dingy and smelling of mold. There were no windows; what little light splayed across the concrete walls and floor came from a strip of fluorescent lights running across the ceiling, but even if the place had been lit up like a Christmas tree, there would have been nothing to see.

"Talk about no frills," Jeremy commented. "Maybe a potted plant in the corner? Spruce the place up a bit?"

"I don't think they get many visitors," Janice said, as she moved beside Charlie into the room. "It's not exactly on the Freedom Trail."

Rod and his mother, a harried but kind-looking woman with the same jet-black hair as her son, were still behind them down the hallway that led to the elevators, and three floors up, to the front entrance of the municipal building at the corner of Government Center. It was the kind of building you might walk past a dozen times and never wonder what was inside. Concrete, square, rising five stories above a plaza that was equally stark and stone, the building had windows covered by bars and a roof flat enough to land a plane. But, as Marion had explained when they'd first met Rod and Nina Lopez outside her place of work, you couldn't expect much more from a style of architecture known as "brutalist."

"The term actually comes from a French word for raw concrete," Marion had said, as Rod had explained to his mother why they were there. "The idea is to provide a massive, fortresslike feeling."

As Nina Lopez had led them through the lobby of the building and then to the elevators that led down into its depths, Marion had continued his lecture, even though nobody had asked him. In the elevator, he had a large captive audience—all the Whiz Kids, Alice Yang, Janice, Rod, and Rod's mother; there was no way he was going to miss out on an opportunity to talk about architecture.

"This building, and much of City Hall, was designed

in 1963, at the height of the brutalist movement, by three architects named Kallmann, McKinnell, and Knowles. When this building went up, some people complained that they were trying to mimic Stalinist Russia, but I think it's more Minecraft than Moscow."

Rod had shaken his head as the elevator reached the basement level, depositing them in the hallway that had led them to the cell-like room they now inhabited.

"You might be the nerdiest of nerds," he said, but then his mother shot him a look, and he actually apologized.

Charlie grinned inwardly; it was nice having Rod's mother along, and not just because she was the key to what came next.

Charlie wasn't sure when, exactly, he had first remembered noticing the "eye in the sky," the little video camera. But once he'd realized that the camera affixed to that ancient lamp might be the break they were looking for, he'd immediately thought of Rod's mother.

Janice had told him she was the head of security at a Boston municipal building; it hadn't been much of a stretch to think that she might be able to get them to the main surveillance center of the Boston Parks Department. And, indeed, once Janice had convinced Rod to ask her, she'd been more than happy to help.

Maybe she felt a little guilty that she worked so many long hours and that Rod was often on his own; or maybe she was just happy that Rod was finally playing well with others, something that certainly didn't come easy to the big kid. But once Charlie, with the help of Marion, had tracked down where the footage from the security camera in the Public Garden was stored, she had made the necessary phone calls to get them access to the central surveillance storage facility.

"This is what we call ground zero," Nina Lopez said as she entered the room next to her son. "It's the center of the intricate web of cameras that keep watch over the public places in Boston."

Nina had the same good looks as her son—not just the hair, so fine like silk that you could see every strand, but also high cheekbones, a Roman nose, and eyes that were perfect ellipses. When they'd first met, Alice Yang had told the security manager that she could have easily been on TV; Nina had laughed at the notion.

"I enjoy my work too much to do anything else," she'd said. "A lot of the time, it's pretty slow—just watching the world go by through thousands of eyes— but sometimes you get to help people, and that makes it all worth it. A week ago we caught a robbery in progress in the Fens, and two days before that we found a lost kid wandering along the Esplanade. If we hadn't been watching, he might have fallen right in the Charles."

She crossed the small room to a bank of black-and-white monitors that sat on a small desk by the far wall. Next to the desk were rows of filing cabinets, marked by designations Charlie couldn't begin to understand. But, luckily, Nina was fluent in municipal scrawl; she quickly found what she was looking for and yanked one of the cabinets open to reveal rows of black plastic USB flash drives.

"These are all from the cameras in the Public Garden, and each of these drives has twenty-four hours of footage on it. I hope you have a date and time in mind, because otherwise we're going to be here all night."

Charlie closed his eyes, numbers floating through his head. This wasn't high-level math, but it was high stakes. He counted backward from the current date, and then made an educated guess. The piece of tusk they'd found in the Public Garden couldn't have been there very long or someone else would have stumbled upon it. He figured they should start with the night before he and his friends had gone on their field trip, and work back from there.

After he gave Nina the date, she went through the row of black chips, her sinewy fingers running along the rows until they landed on a drive in the middle, halfway down. She grabbed the chip, then turned to one of the monitors, deftly locating the chip reader. Once she'd inserted it, the monitor crackled to life, and the screen flickered, filled with fuzzy white snow.

A moment later the snow was replaced by a black-and-white image captured from above: In one distant corner, Charlie could see the small bronze Make Way for Ducklings sculptures and the rolling paths that led from the baby ducks all the way to the area he remembered, where he and his friends had found the tusk. As he watched, a time stamp ran along at the top of the screen, the minutes moving fast, time speeding up.

A handful of people went by, limbs jerking strangely in the sped-up flow of time. Charlie saw a few strollers pushed by nannies, then a couple, then a pack of kids in uniforms. Then, according to the time stamp, it got later.

It was obviously night; moonlight played across the snowy grass, and errant branches twitched like skeletal fingers through the dim cones of light from the electric lamps.

"Fast-forward," Kentaro said. "Nothing is happening."

"Give it time," Alice Yang said. She was leaning close to the monitor, blocking some of Charlie's view. "Most of investigative work is just being patient."

As the time stamp read midnight, the park looked frozen and empty, more like a photo than video from a surveillance camera.

"Maybe we can goose this a little," Nina said, touching a key at the bottom of the monitor.

The scene flickered, time moving faster, and then Charlie saw two forms whizzing across the screen.

"Hold on!" he said. "Back up."

Nina touched another key, and the footage moved backward until it reached the moment when the two forms reappeared, moving to the same spot where Charlie and his friends had been digging.

"Well, look at that," Janice said, and whistled. "Two a.m."

From above, it was hard to tell, but the two forms looked like men. At first they were just strolling by, but then they slowed to a stop. They seemed to be waiting for someone, and a few clicks of sped-up time later, that someone arrived: a third form, coming from the other direction.

"Can we zoom in on them?" Charlie asked. He could feel the adrenalin moving through him. Three men, meeting in the exact spot where he and his friends had found the fragment of woolly mammoth tusk. It couldn't be a coincidence.

Rod's mom turned a knob that looked like a toy joystick. As she maneuvered the little plastic ball, twisting it slowly, the picture became more grainy and the forms on the screen grew larger. As the grainy footage came into focus, Charlie's mouth went dry.

Even from above he had no trouble recognizing Gareth and Grill, Headstrom's "associates." Gareth's square figure took up almost twice as many pixels on the screen as his insectlike cohort. The third man was a mystery; he looked to be wearing an overcoat and a fur Russian-style hat, and Charlie saw that he was carrying a briefcase. When he looked closer, he saw that Grill was also holding a similar briefcase.

"This doesn't look kosher," Crystal murmured. "Who meets like this in a park in the middle of the night?"

Before anyone could answer, the unknown man in the overcoat held out the briefcase. Gareth took the case, and then Grill handed his own briefcase to the unknown man. The unknown man looked like he was about to walk away, then thought better of it and paused, saying something to the two henchmen. There was another pause, then Grill nodded and the unknown man bent down on one knee, carefully opening the case he had just gotten from Headstrom's man.

Everyone in the surveillance room leaned forward to try to get a look into the open case. It was hard to know for sure, but Charlie thought he could make out a pile of what looked to be narrow, bonelike objects.

"Do you think that's—" he started to ask, when suddenly all three men on the screen looked to their right, as if something had startled them. The man down on one knee nearly toppled over at the motion, and something fell out of his case, landing on the ground by his feet.

The man hastily closed the case on the remaining items, then started sweeping his hands around him, obviously looking for the object that had fallen out. Gareth and Grill shouted something at him, then turned and headed quickly out of the picture. The man on his knees gave it another few seconds, then quickly got to his feet as well and took off.

There was a moment of static screen, then a few seconds later a policeman came into view, strolling through the park on what was obviously his regular beat. He passed right by where the three men had met, then kept going. Then the screen was empty again, save for the snow, the trees. Charlie squinted as hard as he could, but he could not make out the object that had fallen out of the unknown man's case; when he'd swept his hands around searching for it, he must have buried it—just enough for a bunch of kids to dig it up the next day.

Rod's mother took the chip out of the monitor, then held it in her hands.

"I'm not sure what we just saw, but I'll keep this key in a secure place, just in case we need it for evidence."

Charlie nodded. Although nothing they'd seen was clear evidence of anything illegal, it was pretty suspicious. Headstrom's associates had given a briefcase full of objects to a man in exchange for something else, in another briefcase. One of those objects had fallen out, and the next day Marion had dug up a fragment of woolly mammoth tusk from that very same spot.

"He's selling mammoth tusk?" Alice Yang said, breaking the silence. "But there's nothing illegal about that. Why do it in a park, in the middle of the night?"

Charlie stared at the monitor, which was now showing nothing but static.

"Curious and curiouser," he said.

15

THE NEXT TWENTY-FOUR HOURS were the longest of Charlie's life. Everyone knew that there was no time slower than the minutes marked by a clock hanging from a classroom wall; but that particular Thursday, Nagassack Middle was giving Charlie an excruciating lesson in Einstein's theory of relativity. From the moment of the first bell, when he and Jeremy had trudged off to morning homeroom, through the forty-minute lunch period, when he and the rest of his Whiz Kids had tried their best to avoid all the pitfalls of sixth grade, Charlie had his mind on one thing. It wasn't chance encounters with Dylan and his crew, or avoiding the potential handing out of extra homework by an overeager teacher, or even the possibility of a bad meatball causing stomach issues that could land a kid in the nurse's office. It was that video surveillance footage. Charlie couldn't risk any of these things getting in the way, because after what he'd seen on the footage the night before, he was more determined than ever to see this through to the end.

He felt certain that Headstrom was up to something nefarious; the image of those two "associates" and their meeting in the park in the middle of the night was hard to shake. Even if they were selling legal mammoth ivory, it was still suspicious. That was something you could do right out in the open. And, anyway, Headstrom had said he was a collector of mammoth ivory, not a distributor. It just didn't make any sense.

When, finally, the bell rang to signify the end of another school day, Charlie was ready to climb the walls. He was almost jogging when he met Jeremy by their lockers. His friend was putting books, gym socks, and god only knows what else into his backpack, moving at such a frantic pace that Charlie could see his friend was as eager to get back to their investigation as he was.

"Don't forget the kitchen sink," Charlie said, as Jeremy jammed more items into the front pocket of his pack. "That thing's going to explode if you don't watch out. You're a real hoarder, you know that?"

Jeremy grabbed a final handful from his locker,

stuffing it into the pack. As he tried to close the zipper, a few items clattered to the floor. Charlie bent down to help his friend pick them up: a fidget spinner, two plastic spiders, and a tube of some sort of cream.

"I think that's Marion's," Jeremy said, pointing to the cream. "Probably for some horrible skin allergy we don't want to know anything about."

Charlie stuffed the tube into his pocket, figuring he would return it to Marion before the kid blew up like a puffer fish from whatever allergen the cream was designed to fight. Then he gestured for his friend to hurry.

"I'm sure Janice and Rod are already on their way to Church's lab," he said. "They get out of school twenty minutes before we do."

"So?" Jeremy asked. "You think they'll have cured cancer before we get there?"

Charlie laughed.

"Well, Dr. Church says the only law his students aren't allowed to break is the First Law of Thermodynamics. And the motto of the lab is 'Nothing is impossible.'"

Students and postdocs pirouetted by, carrying pipettes, test tubes, and DNA trays, a constant ballet of motion—business as usual, but to Charlie it was a thing of wonder, watching genius at work. He knew that at this very moment these young scientists were chasing adventures of their own, seeking cures to diseases such as cancer and Alzheimer's, trying to help people all over the world. Charlie was thrilled to be a part of this, even if the mammals he was trying to save weighed thousands of pounds and had trunks instead of noses.

He was gathered with his friends, new and old—Janice and Rod, next to Jeremy, Crystal, Marion, and Kentaro—in an open corner of the lab. Alice Yang had been planning to join them, but as a high school student, she wouldn't get out of classes for at least another hour. Church was already on his feet in front of them, holding the fragment of tusk that Charlie had given him at the lecture—the sample that Crystal had swiped from the table at Headstrom's construction site.

"Headstrom was correct when he explained the Schreger lines to you," Church was saying. "Those markings do help us determine if a tusk is mammoth or elephant. As it turns out, those lines have to do with the relative density of the dentinal tubules."

The words seemed hard to pronounce, let alone understand.

"'Dentinal tubules'?" Jeremy said. "Sounds like some sort of gum."

"'Dentinal' does mean 'of the dentin,' which is the

main ingredient that makes up teeth, and where Dentyne gum got its name. Tubules are little microscopic tubes that run through teeth, and tusks. Tusks really are just overgrown canines, like the sharp side teeth in a dog's mouth, or even in ours."

Church bared his teeth to show off his own tiny canines. The kids were shocked to see how undersized Dr. Church's teeth were for a man of such stature.

He closed his lips, then continued:

"A high density of tubules, like those found in ancient mammoth tusks, creates a cross section of lines that form a more acute angle. Consequently, mammoth Schreger lines look like little teepees, whereas the Schreger lines of an elephant's tusk look more obtuse, like a flattened-out, wide triangle."

Church made his way through the circle of kids and grabbed his laptop, which sat on a nearby bench, then fiddled with the keys on the keyboard. Suddenly, a white light was projected out of a device attached to the computer, and an image appeared on the wall across the lab. The image was circular, a cross section of tusk, and through the circle Charlie could see lines forming a perfectly obtuse angle. There was no doubt; the lines came together in an angle greater than a hundred degrees.

Even though it wasn't necessary, Crystal grabbed a protractor from Jeremy's backpack and approached the image. She opened up the hinge of the tool and lined up the arms with the lines on the image.

"One hundred and five degrees. Definitely obtuse."

There was a pause, then Janice spoke.

"Definitely elephant, not mammoth." Then she looked at Charlie.

"The tusk from Headstrom's construction site is illegal elephant ivory. That means he lied. The one in his office might be mammoth, but this one is clearly elephant."

"It's not surprising," Church said. "Mammoth ivory is still pretty rare. Elephants are killed every day for their ivory, even though the trade became illegal back in 1999. More than thirty thousand elephants are killed every year by poachers, and millions of dollars' worth of ivory changes hands every month. You can walk into any jewelry store in Chinatown and buy elephant ivory. In fact, up until recently, even pianos were made with elephant ivory in their keys. That's why playing the piano is sometimes called "tickling the ivories.""

Church retrieved the piece of elephant tusk from the desk near his computer and handed it to Charlie.

"I think Headstrom is doing more than tickling

this ivory," Charlie said. "I think he's selling it in cities across the country and funding his savanna projects with the profits."

"That's quite an accusation," Dr. Church said. "You're going to need some good evidence to back it up. One tusk from a construction site isn't going to be enough."

Suddenly, Charlie noticed that Marion was rustling in his own backpack, which was beneath his chair. Carefully, he removed the plaster boot-print cast that Crystal had given him to scan. Along with the cast, he had a bunch of printed pages of computer paper.

He held up one of the pages. On the paper was a scanned image of the boot print, covered in lines and notations, along with a bar graph at the bottom.

"You triangulated a boot print?" Jeremy asked.

"Not exactly. I actually used some pretty cool recognition software to match points on the boot with a database of every type of boot sold in the past three years. Although it's not a perfect match, I believe this particular brand of boot is worn by boat crews and wharf workers, mostly cargo crews manning long-voyage cargo ships."

Charlie raised his eyebrows.

"So the man who met Headstrom's henchmen at the

Public Garden was wearing wharf boots? Why would he be wearing wharf boots?"

"I think it's fairly elementary," Janice said. "And I'm pretty sure if we follow those boots, we aren't going to find any Hello Kitty imprints above the heels."

No, Charlie thought to himself. *If we're lucky, we'll find something much more valuable—and enough to stop Headstrom in his tracks.*

16

THE SKY HAD TURNED gunmetal gray by the time Charlie, Jeremy, Marion, and Kentaro followed Crystal, Janice, and Rod along the ramp that led down the backside of the Conley Container Terminal. They were deep in the heart of the seaport. From up close, the Container Terminal was a long, boxy warehouse that looked itself like an enormous boot set down onto the pier by a drunken giant, tilted at an angle along the water, with multiple docks extending outward like toes sticking out from holes torn down the sole.

Briny air filled Charlie's nostrils as he moved slowly down the ramp. He could hear the soft creak of Janice's wheelchair as she led them all forward, and he was amazed at how calm and fearless she seemed. Inside, he was terrified. He knew they should have called one of their parents to come with them, rather than letting Rod order them a pair of Ubers using his mother's phone. At the very least, they should have waited for Alice Yang to show up at Church's lab to go with them down to the docks. She wasn't quite an adult, but she could pass— and the truth was, Charlie had never felt more like a kid than at that very moment.

He had been in plenty of dangerous situations before. He'd taken down an amusement park using math, with the help of a mysterious group of seventh graders, and had narrowly escaped the clutches of some extremely tough characters in the process. Likewise, he'd faced danger and betrayal in the quest to find moon rocks that had gone missing from NASA. But this felt different. This was a mystery he and his friends had followed on their own from beginning to end, and now they were really alone, just a few feet from the frozen water of Boston Harbor. This wasn't just dangerous, it was a little bit insane.

He looked past Janice to the behemoth cargo ships that dotted the water ahead of him. Between the ships, he counted a dozen blue and white cranes stretching into the gray sky, looking a lot like *Star Wars* AT-AT walkers. He knew the cranes were used to move massive rectangular containers onto the ships. Each container was at least the size of a small car, and some were big enough that people had begun converting them into makeshift houses.

Above the cranes, a plane soared toward Logan Airport, which sat kitty-corner to the farthest pier. Even though the airport was at least a mile away, Charlie could hear the roar of the airplane's engine.

"Hold on a second," Crystal said, as she stopped near the bottom of the ramp. To her right was an equipment rack, and Charlie saw that one shelf was nearly covered in a pile of bright yellow life jackets.

Crystal grabbed one of the life jackets, then handed it to Charlie.

"Can't be too careful," she said, and she then took more jackets off the shelf and tossed them to Jeremy, Kentaro, Rod, and Marion.

"I think I'm going to stay away from the water," Janice said when Crystal handed her one as well. "My chair never passed its swimming test."

"I think this looks pretty good," Kentaro said, as he slung his vest over his shoulders. "Anything neon gets a gold star from me."

Charlie put his own vest on. The clasps in the front gave him a bit of trouble, but before he could figure them out, Janice had rolled around to face him and was doing the clasps with her fingers.

"The trick is to not be a clumsy oaf," she said, grinning. As she was doing the clasps, she noticed that Charlie's fingers were shaking, and she pointed to her chair. "We're going to be fine. Don't forget, I've got my trusty magic wand."

Charlie blushed. When everyone was done putting on their jackets, they all turned back to face the dock.

A loud beeping noise went off and Rod quickly reached for his pocket.

"Wow, that's one way to get us noticed!" Kentaro whispered.

Rod pulled out the phone and quickly turned the ringer off, but not before reading the message on the screen. He knew he was probably going to regret having grabbed it from his mother's purse earlier. He looked down and saw the message: ROD, IT'S MOM. I KNOW YOU HAVE MY PHONE. It was clear from the all caps letters from an unknown number that he was going to be in big trouble later. But that was the least of his worries.

"Yeah, it was dumb to take my mom's phone, but how else would we have gotten here?"

"Good point," Charlie said.

"Where do we go next?" Rod asked. "I mean, I like the sea air as much as the next guy. But there are a lot of boats to search in this place. I see four on this dock alone, and how do we even know that we're on the right dock?"

"We're on the right dock," Crystal said. She was suddenly standing a step back from the rest, scanning the nearby boats, which rose up from the water almost like mountains. A few of them were at least four stories high, with portholes running behind the cargo cranes. "And better yet, I know exactly what boat we're looking for."

Charlie stared at her. She'd been quiet during the Uber ride from Dr. Church's lab, and now that he thought about it, he realized she'd been on Rod's mother's phone for at least part of the trip.

"Google Earth," she said, smiling. "It's pretty handy when you're looking for something big. The bigger, the better."

She reached out and pointed to one of the boats, about fifty yards away down the dock. The boat looked to be about half a football field in length, rising up four stories, to a wide deck half-filled with crates. Next to the boat was one of the cargo cranes—a contraption made up of pulleys and ballasts. At the moment a large crate was rising halfway up the ship, being lifted by the crane; two ropes were wrapped around the crate, leading up over a pulley, then down to a huge ballast—a weight— that was being lowered by an automated crank. Someone was obviously controlling the crank from somewhere on the ship. Next to the crane, more crates were piled up a good ten yards across the dock.

"How do you know we're looking for that ship? All we have is a boot print."

Crystal grinned.

"That's not all we have. We also have our memories. A specific memory, actually. You were there, Charlie. You too, Kentaro."

Charlie racked his brain. The only place he'd been alone with Crystal and Kentaro was when they'd tried—and failed—to sneak into the savanna exhibit. He tried to picture the moment: how they'd been stopped trying to climb the fence, the walk over to the domed construct in the middle of the site, the conversation with Headstrom. The spinning globe, the piece of tusk on the desk. Next to the piece of tusk . . .

Charlie stared at the giant ship, looking past the crane, up toward the deck. A few feet from the highest railing he saw the printed letters of the ship's name.

"The *London Fog*," he read out loud.

"The coffee cup," Kentaro said. "The way it was facing us, I could only read a few letters: LON."

"It wasn't that tough to figure out the rest," Crystal said. "I mean, all I had to do was look on Google Earth to see what ships happened to be in the harbor, take down their names, then see what matched. I guess I got lucky."

"Luck had nothing to do with it," Janice said. "Like I said, you're freaking Batman."

Rod took a step down the ramp.

"Let's go see what we can find."

"Hold on," Charlie said. "We can't all go marching down there; someone is going to see us. We need to split up. Jeremy, Crystal, and I will head toward the front of the boat and check out those crates. Marion and Rod, you guys go to the back, see if anything is around that side. Kentaro, you and Janice stay back here. That way Janice can stay farther from the water, and if you see anything suspicious, make a sound like a seagull."

"What does a seagull sound like?" Janice asked, as the groups started forward.

"It sounds a lot like a little Japanese kid screaming for his life," Kentaro said, grinning.

Fifteen minutes later Charlie was following Jeremy and Crystal along the side of the massive ship, slowly closing in on the pile of crates beside the automated crane. From up close, the ship seemed impossibly large; even on his toes, Charlie couldn't see the top. The smell of ocean and fish and brine was so thick in his nose that it made him want to gag, and the dock was slippery with water beneath his feet, but he was determined to see this through.

Each step brought him closer to the crates, and that crane, which was whirring along, the ballast slowly lowering as yet another huge parcel began lifting off the ground. The crates must have been extremely heavy; doing the calculations in his head, Charlie knew that the crane could lift an enormous amount of weight, but even so, the crate attached to the rigging was moving just inches at a time, swinging slightly back and forth. No doubt when it reached the deck thirty feet above, it would take more than one man to unload it from the ropes.

The boat must have had a crew in the dozens—maybe including at least one crew member who had made a trip to the Public Garden two weeks earlier, in the middle of the night. A trip that involved the exchange of suitcases and a dropped slice of mammoth tusk.

A few more feet and then Crystal and Jeremy stopped. They had reached the closest crate.

"It's about six feet long," Crystal said, measuring with her eyes, "maybe half as high."

She reached forward with both hands and touched the top. The crate was closed, but there were latches along the wood. Without pause, Crystal went at the latches, and in less than a minute she had them all undone.

"Here we go," she said, and then beckoned Jeremy and Charlie to help.

Together, they all pushed at the wood, and the top swung open.

Charlie gasped.

Below the lid was a perfect line of tusks, each around four feet long, carefully packed into the crate in a bed of beige packing straw.

Without a word, Charlie reached in and took hold of one of the tusks. It was heavy, at least twenty pounds, appeared to have been sheared at the base in a single, flat stroke. With Jeremy's help, he lifted the tusk out of the crate and turned it on its side. Crystal moved close to the base, peering at what looked like hatched lines within the circular cut. She quickly grabbed her pocket magnifying glass from her bag and held it up to the sample.

Then her face seemed to fall.

"Teepees," she said. "This is a mammoth tusk."

Charlie stared at her.

"That's not possible," he said. "These can't be mammoth."

"Look for yourself."

Charlie leaned the tusk against the side of the crate and looked. She was right—clearly, the Schreger lines came together in a ninety-degree angle. Mammoth. Whoever was moving these crates of ivory wasn't breaking the law. If Headstrom was linked to this boat, he had been telling the truth.

Charlie shook his head.

"It can't be. It just can't," he said, and he banged his hand against the crate.

There was a rumble as the contents of the crate shifted downward. Charlie saw that Jeremy was peering into the open top, and followed his gaze. The top layer of tusks had rolled to one side, revealing another layer beneath. The second layer wasn't packed anywhere near as nicely as the top, and as Charlie looked deeper, he could see that there were more layers beneath, all the way to the bottom of the crate. More tusks—many more tusks.

With Jeremy's help, Charlie reached into the crate and pulled out one of the lower tusks. Once it was free, he held the base toward Crystal. Her eyes went wide.

"Obtuse angles," she said. "This isn't mammoth. This is elephant."

Charlie put the tusk down and reached into the crate

again, lifting out another sample. Again, he showed it to Crystal.

"Elephant!" she said.

Another tusk—and the same result.

"These are all elephant! Just the top layer is mammoth. If this holds for the rest of these crates—there has to be hundreds of pounds of elephant ivory in here. Being loaded onto this ship to sell god knows where."

Charlie exhaled.

"He's camouflaging his elephant ivory with mammoth tusks. Most people can't tell the difference. So he gets a few mammoth tusks in case anyone takes a closer look, keeps them on top—but the rest is all elephant. He must have been making a deal in the park; one of the top tusks fell out of the suitcase, but the rest would have all been elephant. Headstrom is an illegal ivory trader. That's how he's funding his savannas."

Before Charlie could say any more, loud cawing sounds erupted from the back; it was the strangest-sounding bird Charlie had ever heard. He realized, with a start, that it wasn't a bird at all.

It was a terrified Japanese kid.

Before Charlie could move, he felt two pawlike hands come down hard against his shoulders. Without thinking, he grabbed one of the elephant tusks in both hands, and swung around with all his strength. The tusk connected with a meaty shoulder, and the hands released. Charlie saw Gareth staggering backward, slamming right into Grill, who lost his footing on the wet dock and fell right on his rump.

"KID," Grill snarled. "I think you tore my favorite pants."

Charlie's heart rocketed in his chest. He saw Crystal and Jeremy scattering in different directions, and realized he had to move too, because Gareth was already helping Grill back to his feet, and then they were both coming forward.

Charlie held the tusk in front of him in both hands like a baseball bat.

"I don't want to have to use this," he said, trying to sound menacing. The two thugs laughed in harmony.

"Go ahead," Gareth said, his teeth like dominoes in his mouth. "First swing is free. Second swing is gonna cost you."

Charlie backed up, past the crate, then kept backing up, heels first. He could hear the whirring of the crane getting louder, and realized he was just a few feet away. The rising crate was about waist high and starting to move faster now that it was no longer on the ground.

He made a split-second decision and spun away

from the two thugs. Then he was moving at full speed toward the hanging crate. With a howl he leaped up onto it. His weight sent the wooden box swinging forward into a high arc—then Newton's Third Law of Motion took over.

"Every action has an equal and opposite reaction!" Charlie yelled, as the crate swung back toward the two thugs, who were trying desperately to stop their own forward motion across the slippery deck.

With a thud, the box slammed into Gareth's chest, sending him sprawling back into Grill, who again hit the dock with a solid boom.

Then Charlie was rising up the side of the boat, faster and faster, fighting for balance against the swinging of the wooden box, the elephant tusk still in his hands.

He could hear the two thugs shouting at him from below, but he was focused on the ship's deck, which was rapidly getting closer. Another few seconds and the crane was lifting his crate over the edge. He saw a wide-open area of deck, surrounded by boxes piled high, and at least four men in heavy coats and gloves. One of the men saw him on top of the crate and pointed—but Charlie didn't wait for the rest to notice him.

As soon as the teetering box was over the deck, he

leaped off the side, hitting the wood with both feet. Then he was racing forward, trying to find somewhere to go. He saw a door leading deeper into the boat, and he grabbed at the knob. Then he was moving through a long hallway.

The hallway ended at another door. Charlie slowed his gait, trying to come up with some sort of plan. He knew by now the two thugs would be making their way through the ship. They wouldn't have been able to take an easy way to the top as he had, but they would be there soon enough. Charlie hoped that the rest of his friends had gotten away. Maybe Rod had called the police. But Charlie knew that for the moment he was on his own.

The door led into a cramped galley—walls lined with metal ovens, shelves lined with pots and pans. Down the center of the galley, larger pans hung from a long metal rack along the ceiling. Charlie moved quickly below the pans, heading for a door on the other side.

Just as he reached the second door, he heard footsteps.

He turned to see Gareth coming into the galley, his huge form taking up most of the narrow alley leading between the ovens and shelves. Grill was behind him. Grill's sleeves looked torn and tattered from his fall to the deck, and though Charlie couldn't see the man's pants, he assumed they were ruined as well.

"You're in a lot of trouble," the insectoid thug sneered. "But if you drop the tusk, maybe we'll let you go."

Charlie glanced at the tusk in his hands. He knew he couldn't drop it—it was elephant ivory, evidence that could bring Headstrom down. Charlie was sure that once this ship was impounded, the police would easily be able to link Headstrom to the crates of ivory on the deck and the dock, with the help of the video Rod's mom had locked in a municipal safe.

Charlie couldn't give up the tusk that easily; it was actually going to be part of his master plan.

He glanced up above his head, to the metal rack that ran along the ceiling, holding up all those heavy pots and pans.

Then he looked back at the two men moving toward him, right below all that cooking hardware.

"Sorry, guys, but it looks like rain."

Charlie slammed the tusk up above his head, aiming the tip right into the metal rack. There was a loud crash of ivory against metal, and then the pots and pans came tumbling down, right on top of the two henchmen. Gareth and Grill screamed in unison, and then

Charlie was moving forward again, through the second doorway.

He saw a narrow stairway and decided he had no choice. He didn't want to be going up, but there was no way down.

A minute later he burst out onto the bow of the enormous boat. The area in front of him was vaguely triangular, with a wooden floor and a waist-high railing around the edges. As he moved forward, he realized that there was nowhere to go. He was at the very peak of the boat, and beyond the railing, there was nothing separating him from a long drop down to the water.

"I think you miscalculated," said a voice from behind.

Charlie turned to see Grill coming out of the stairwell, followed by his bulky companion.

Charlie shivered, then headed to the railing, and shaking from head to toe, he began to climb over.

A second later he was on the other side, his shoes on the lip of the boat, his toes hanging out over the plunge down to the harbor.

17

"I MIGHT BE CRAZY," Charlie said, "but I never miscalculate."

He stepped off the edge of the deck, and suddenly he was plummeting toward the icy water below.

Seconds later he hit the water feetfirst. The shock of the cold ricocheted through his body, starting at his feet and caterwauling all the way to the top of his skull. His chest seized, his lungs filled with daggers, and his legs flailed back and forth as the cold harbor engulfed him, pulling him down, deeper and deeper.

His eyes clenched shut, heck, everything on him clenched, clenched, clenched. His mouth was sealed tight, holding his breath against the icy water that lapped at his face. His arms were like steel springs, clutching the tusk hard against the front of his neon vest. He could feel all the muscles in his body twitching as the icy water tore at him, but the skin of his face, his fingers, his wrists, wherever he'd rubbed the lotion from the tube in his pocket, felt somehow protected. He knew in the part of his brain that was still functioning that the feeling wouldn't last. But then, before the thought even finished coalescing, he was moving up, up, up, carried by the internal padding of the vest, the difference in density and volume gifting buoyancy, wonderful, miraculous buoyancy.

And then his head burst free from the water and he was sucking in air, thrashing with his feet.

Two seconds later he felt himself being lifted even higher, and then he was banging down against the dock, water running off him in heavy drops. He looked up and saw Rod standing next to Alice Yang. Rod still had a strong grip on the back of Charlie's vest, holding him up on his knees.

Charlie shivered intensely as Rod let him go, sending him collapsing against the dock, his fingers still wrapped around the tusk. Alice Yang hovered over him, Rod's mother's cell phone in her hands.

"The police will be here in a minute," she said. "I got here just in time to see you take that leap. You could have frozen to death."

Charlie could see the rest of his friends running toward them from their hiding places along the pier. Crystal and Jeremy were closest, maybe ten yards away, followed by Kentaro and Marion. He could also see Janice rolling down the ramp.

"I had a little help," Charlie said, pointing toward his pocket. "A tube of one of Marion's skin creams. Most skin creams have a Vaseline, or similar, paraffin-like base. Paraffins can enhance skin protection by a factor of nearly two point five. Not as good as a diver's suit, but it worked well enough in a pinch."

"You've got to be the coolest nerd I've ever met," Rod started to say, when suddenly Charlie saw a shape move forward from behind a nearby crate.

To his shock, Charlie recognized Blake Headstrom, strolling toward him in a white windbreaker that matched his ice-blond hair, as if he didn't have a care in the world. Before anyone could react, Headstrom side-stepped between Rod and Alice, and grabbed the tusk out of Charlie's frozen grip.

"Glad I keep close tabs on my associates," Headstrom said. "Good help is hard to find. People like Gareth and Grill tend more toward brawn than brains."

And just as suddenly he was walking away toward

the boat, the tusk tucked under one arm. Charlie reached after him, but his legs were barely working. Rod took a step, but Alice grabbed his arm.

"What are you going to do, tackle him? He'll have you arrested."

"He's holding an elephant tusk," Rod shouted. But Alice shook her head.

"By the time anyone figures that out you'll be half-way to juvenile hall."

"But he's walking away with the evidence," Charlie mumbled.

Jeremy and Crystal arrived by his side, breathing hard, followed by Marion and Kentaro. They were all still watching Headstrom, who had made it to a ramp leading up to the back entrance to the ship, when Janice wheeled up right next to Charlie, looking down at him, concern in her eyes.

"Are you okay?" she asked.

Charlie shook his head. There were frozen tears in the corners of his eyes.

"All that—for nothing. He'll get rid of everything. He'll get away with everything."

For some reason, Janice didn't look upset. In fact, she was smiling.

She reached down into her chair, to where the wheel met the metal, and retrieved something small, curved, and white.

"It was the littlest one I could find," she said.

It was a tusk.

"How?" was all Charlie could manage.

"I came down and took it from one of the crates while all of you were busy being heroic. See, nobody notices the girl in the wheelchair."

"Your magic wand," Charlie said.

Janice laughed.

"Sometimes," she said, holding the little tusk above her head. "And now we're going to wave it and make the bad guy disappear."

"INCOMING!"

Charlie's instincts kicked in and he dived for the carpeted floor of his family's basement rec room. He nearly upended the low wooden coffee table with legs shaped like sea horses that sat in front of the kidney-shaped five-seater couch his parents had picked up at a furniture warehouse in Vermont. He finally looked up and realized he wasn't dodging a pipette filled with liquid or a football or any other hurled projectile, and a smile spread across his face.

Rod grinned back at him from above the tray of nachos, which the big kid then carefully placed on the coffee table, just inches from Charlie's prone form.

"We've really got to work on that if we're going to

be hanging out," Rod said with a chuckle. "I mean, you can't be diving for the floor every time I come into the room. It's unseemly."

Charlie blushed. A lot had happened in the week that had passed since Rod had plucked Charlie out of the harbor, and Janice had saved the day with the hidden tusk.

Although Charlie had felt fine, when the police finally arrived, they whisked him right to Children's Hospital for a quick checkup. As he'd calculated, the tube of Marion's skin cream he'd taken from Jeremy's backpack had saved him from even the slightest case of frostbite. All he'd suffered from his quick dip in the icy waters was a minor headache that had lasted less than half a day.

In fact, the headache had been a distant memory by the time the police finished interviewing him, and the rest of his friends. At first the detectives had been skeptical about what they were hearing. But when Rod's mother showed up with the video evidence of the clandestine meeting in the Public Garden, everything had changed. Although it would take time, the detectives had agreed to take over the investigation from Charlie and his friends. Further, the detective had thanked Charlie for his help, and told him that when all the dust settled, he felt sure that the mayor was going to give the Whiz Kids a commendation. It wasn't every day that an illegal ivory trader was brought down in Boston, by a group of overly smart kids.

Janice wheeled next to Charlie and offered a hand, helping him back to the couch. Jeremy and Crystal made room for him, just as Marion shouted at them to pay attention, pointing to the TV, which was lodged in a wooden cabinet at the head of the room. A banner had appeared across the television, with the Channel 7 logo right in the middle, followed by the words "Spotlight Exclusive."

Kentaro came running down the stairs, his little legs spinning like the rotors of a motorboat.

"Is it starting?"

"I think this is it!" Jeremy said.

Charlie focused again on the TV. Although his parents were upstairs in the living room, giving Charlie and his friends free reign in the basement, Charlie knew they were watching as well. They hadn't been thrilled when they'd first heard what Charlie and his friends had been up to over the past couple of weeks. When they'd picked him up from the hospital, they were both terrified to find out about his swim in the harbor, and angry that he'd been chasing something so dangerous without their knowledge. But when the detectives had explained the good Charlie and his friends had done by stopping the sale of ivory—and probably saving many elephants in the process—they'd relented. As long as Charlie promised to remain on land for the time being, they were willing to forgive.

Charlie had no intention of going near water again for a long, long time. In fact, the experience had put him off baths; from now on, a quick shower would have to do.

"It's her!" Crystal said.

Charlie watched as the Spotlight banner flickered off the television screen, replaced by Alice Yang, who was standing in the Public Garden, just a few feet away from the bronze Make Way for Ducklings sculpture. She was wearing more makeup than Charlie remembered, and her hair was down around her shoulders. She had also traded her Hello Kitty boots for shiny red shoes. She looked like a reporter, not a high school kid, and when she spoke, she sounded like one too:

"I'm Alice Yang, reporting for the Spotlight Team. Tonight: an investigation involving the illegal trade of elephant ivory, a multimillionaire zoo developer, and the tusk of a woolly mammoth, found right here in the Public Garden by a group of smart, resilient sixth graders."

"Hey, who is she calling resilient?" Jeremy said from the couch.

"It means 'determined,'" Kentaro said.

"I know what it means. But I wasn't resilient; I was scared out of my shorts the whole time."

"Is that why they call you Diapers?" Rod said, and Jeremy shot him a look.

"Will you guys be quiet?" Janice said. "I want to hear this."

Charlie watched as Alice took her television audience through the main beats of the story, from the moment Charlie and his friends had found the woolly mammoth tusk to their discovery of elephant ivory in the crates by the ship docked in Boston Harbor. Although Alice never mentioned any of the Whiz Kids by name, there was no doubt that it was a group of sixth graders who had broken the story. Charlie didn't need the recognition—for him, solving the mystery using science had been more than enough of a reward—but it was cool to hear about himself on TV. Better yet, he was happy to see Alice finally reaching her goal; she looked and sounded like a real reporter, and Charlie was sure this was just the beginning. She was going to follow her sister right into the family business.

"As for Blake Headstrom," Alice was saying, as a

photo of the slick millionaire appeared in the corner of the screen. "He's facing multiple criminal charges as we speak. Yesterday, at a press conference, Headstrom offered a statement."

The screen changed, and suddenly Charlie found himself staring at Headstrom, who was standing in front of a bank of microphones. The man's white-blond hair was perfect, but there seemed to be even more lines on his weathered face.

"There's nothing more important to me than the welfare of the animals in the African savanna, including the noble elephant. Which is why I'll be making a significant donation to the Church Lab, to help with their efforts at studying the elephant's forebears, and their project aimed at resurrecting the woolly mammoth."

The screen cut back to Alice, who offered the slightest hint of a smile.

"No doubt Mr. Headstrom will have plenty of time to contemplate the welfare of the noble elephant when he's officially charged. Signing off, this is Alice Yang, reporting for the Channel 7 Spotlight team."

The screen switched to commercial, and applause erupted through the basement. Charlie felt a hand on his arm, and looked up to see Janice smiling at him from her chair.

"Not bad for a first date, Numbers. You brought down an ivory smuggler and showed me your diving form. You could have stuck the landing a little better, but I still give it an A for effort."

Charlie stared at her.

"F-first date?" he stammered.

"Kidding." She laughed, then she looked at Crystal.

"Is he always like this?"

Crystal smiled.

"Yes, he is."

Then she added:

"But we wouldn't have it any other way."